WITH THIS PLEDGE

Windswept Bay, Book Eight

DEBRA CLOPTON

With This Pledge

After a special ops mission gone terribly wrong, Max Sinclair is home and facing the possibility of losing the career he loves serving his country. When he meets his brother's new stable manager he is drawn to her and feeling more alive.

After a bad situation with her ex-boss, horse trainer Kelsey Malone accepted the job of running the Windswept Bay side stables for Cam Sinclair. She's attracted to his brother Max the moment she sees him at Cam and Lana's engagement party. But her dad was career military and gave his life for his country- Kelsey's vowed she'll never go through that again and doesn't date military men. But things get complicated when her ex-boss shows up and Max steps in to protect her.

Can love heal these two wounded soul's hearts? Welcome back to the beautiful sunset shores of Windswept Bay where the romance continues...

CHAPTER ONE

Kelsey Malone followed the hostess through the packed dining room to the back deck of the Paradise Grill. The beachside restaurant was, from what she'd been told, a favorite gathering spot of Windswept Bay residents and tourists. Tonight was an engagement party for her boss, Cam Sinclair and his bride-to-be, Lana Presley. His family was holding it for him and though the family owned the Windswept Bay Resort, Cam had told Kelsey that they often held family gatherings like this away from the resort.

"Here you go." The hostess pushed open the door.

"The party is on the left side."

"Thank you." Kelsey took a deep breath and stepped out onto the deck. She hadn't been in town that long and she really didn't know anyone well. She knew Cam and Lana and then Levi Sinclair—the chief of police—and his wife, Jessica. She'd been invited to their wedding but in the big picture, she hadn't really been around any of them long enough to actually know them.

But tonight was a chance to start building relationships. That was one of Kelsey's goals when she'd taken this job running the stables for Cam…to start a new life and to basically build a life and settle down. Kelsey had never really had roots anywhere and that was about to change.

Party lights were strung up everywhere and the live band was playing fun, beach, and wedding song inspired music. The moon glistened on the water that could be seen from the deck and she breathed in the salty air. She had quickly fallen in love with the town and the area. Kelsey was a horse trainer and not many ranches were near the beach, so she'd never spent much time in areas such as this. Which meant running a horse riding stable on the beach was a unique opportunity for her and had come at the most perfect and heaven-sent way.

Her gaze found the handsome Cam Sinclair. She felt an overwhelming sense of gratitude to the man who had not listened to gossip and had hired her anyway on her merit and training reputation.

Her gaze shifted to Cam's brother Levi. He and his wife Jessica had been welcoming and wonderful to her. Her gaze was drawn almost immediately to the handsome man beside Levi— There was a seriousness to his look, a solemnness to him. His stance was different; his chest was broader and his biceps thicker with hard, corded muscle. His gaze shifted suddenly and met hers. Instantly, butterflies erupted through her chest. *Goodness.*

"Kelsey."

At the sound of her name, Kelsey yanked her gaze from the man's and found Jessica coming toward her.

"I'm so happy you were able to make it." Jessica hugged her.

"I'm glad to be here," she said, feeling welcomed. "It looks like the party is in full swing. I'm sorry I'm running late. I had a group ride that took longer than expected."

"No worries. Come on, let's move over to the others."

Lana waved to her and motioned for them to head her way. "I'm thrilled that you came. Cam said he thought you were coming."

She told her about the late ride. "It was a great group, though. There was a mixture of adults and children and the kids were adorable. Reminded me of Kevin and Jessica."

Kevin was Jessica's little boy, a first-grader whom she was now giving riding lessons. Kelsey really enjoyed teaching the kids to ride and seeing the excitement in their little faces as they learned the joy of horsemanship.

"You're so good with them," Jessica said.

"Yes, you are and that's why we are so lucky to have you running the stables. It really gives Cam peace of mind when he's in Texas."

No one was happier about her having this job than Kelsey. *She was so grateful for it...for Cam and for Lana*, Kelsey thought once again. She repeated the mantra several times a day.

"Kevin sings your praises all the time. You should hear what he says at school. You'll probably be having some of his classmate's parents calling about lessons."

Kelsey chuckled. "I adore teaching that age. They are a hoot."

"They are a handful." Jessica laughed. "I keep thinking about Levi's mom and dad raising five boys. How did they survive?"

Lana made a humorous face. "Believe me, it probably wasn't easy. I have five brothers myself and I love them but goodness gracious boys are active."

The three of them automatically looked over at the three men talking together.

Kelsey couldn't help but ask, "Who is that talking to Cam and Levi?"

"Oh, you didn't know? That's Max.," Jessica said.

"He looks so serious...or something." She felt instantly embarrassed to let them know she'd looked at

Max that closely.

Lana nodded. "Yes, he's Special Ops with a very elite, and top secret section of the Marines, its kind of like a Navy SEAL. Very dangerous. And Cam said he had been really quiet since coming home. I've not been around him much but I thought the same thing."

"Levi said the exact same thing," Jessica said. "He's quieter. I think he stays to himself more, even when he's home from his missions and not at the base. From what Levi says, he can't talk about his missions even to family. That would be hard, I think."

Kelsey nodded. Thoughts of her dad slammed into her. He had been Special Ops and most of her memories of him were of him being gone and her missing him. She shook off the thoughts and her gaze snagged on Max Sinclair. Instantly, his gaze was back to hers, as if he felt her looking at him. Heat rose up in her body and she hoped the dim lighting hid the flush.

The Sinclair sisters were suddenly there greeting her and she was glad for the distraction.

Cali, Shar, Olivia, and Jillian Sinclair were

friendly and welcoming. They were as nice as they were pretty and Kelsey tried hard to remember who was who. The tall blonde was Cali; she was the oldest and married to a famous artist. The other three were triplets, even though they weren't identical. Shar was dark-headed and the other two looked almost identical.

"Look, girls—I think Max is checking Kelsey out." Shar smiled at her. "Cool."

"Really?" Jillian gasped and shot her brother a glance.

Kelsey was embarrassed and automatically looked his way because everyone else was. He was not looking at her but was focused on something Levi was saying. More guys had joined the group.

"He's been so quiet since he got back," Cali offered, thoughtfully.

"I know. It's driving me crazy," Shar said. "I think something bad happened on that mission. That's why he was gone so long."

"I think so too," Olivia agreed.

"Trent and Max are our quiet brothers and we're

used to that. But Max, has been even more withdrawn since he came home," Jillian explained.

"He can't talk to anyone about the missions," Shar said. "It's just not normal. You need to be able to talk to someone. I know he has his team but still theres something about having family to talk things out with. I worry about him."

Kelsey felt ill at ease discussing Max. And she knew all too well what they were talking about. She didn't want to tell them that if Max was anything like her dad, he was happy with the way his life was. He probably lived every day he was home from a mission ready to go to the next one.

That was how her dad had seemed. Kelsey had lived that life once and would never live that life again. She had a rule: no matter how nice or appealing a man was, if he was in the military of any sort, it turned her off instantly.

Max Sinclair was no different. Yes, she'd felt a reaction when their gazes met but that didn't matter. Nor did it matter whether his sisters thought he might have shown interest in her.

Kelsey did not date military men. Period.

And that fact would never change.

Hours after the party, Max sat in the dark, staring out at the ocean. The white-capped waves rolling in held no candle to the turmoil rolling through him like waves slamming violently against his numb heart.

He was used to being in control of himself—his emotions, his reactions, his thoughts. But tonight he felt as if he were in control of nothing.

He couldn't blank out the loss of his team members. Couldn't relive every move he had made up to the moment that the explosive had been triggered. *Had it been his fault?*

Had two of his friends lost their lives because he'd misread the signs? Because he'd made a mistake?

He really didn't think so, but there was that inkling of doubt.

He rubbed his knee, feeling the swelling and the pain that could at moments rip through him. He fought not to take the painkillers the docs had sent home from the hospital with him. But there had been a few times in the week since he'd arrived home that he'd had to take one. Tonight might end up being one of those nights. He'd had to stand most of the time at his brother's engagement party—it had been hard on his knee. His ACL was torn and the doctors had said it would be good to give the swelling time to go down before considering surgery. He had appointments set up for reevaluation in two weeks. For that and also the verdict about his hearing.

His career was riding on the thin blade of a knife, ready to split either way, and he could do nothing but wait.

He had never been the best at waiting until he'd gone into Special Ops and had to learn patience. But now, this was not about a mission but about him…about whether he would ever be able to go on another mission. He should tell his family. Should let them in on what he was going through. But if any of his family knew that his knee had been torn up on this mission—or that he'd almost been blown up…it was worry and fear that he didn't want to put them through.

That was why he'd kept it a secret. Until he couldn't take the standing any longer and had left early.

Now, he closed his eyes. He lived to protect his country. He had been willing to die to protect his country but it hadn't been him who had died; it had been his team members who had paid the ultimate price. He'd almost missed their funerals and would have if their bodies had made it back sooner. He'd been in the hospital and only released the day before the scheduled funerals.

He knew his brothers—his entire family— wondered why this mission took longer than normal but they didn't know he had spent a week in the hospital recovering. The blast that had killed his two friends had damaged his hearing in his right ear and torn up the interior of his knee on that same side. When that explosive was detonated so close to him, it had sounded as if his head had been inside a steel drum. It had been so loud it was a pure miracle that he had lived—and with almost no visible signs of damage.

Where did he go from here?

As if she could hear his thoughts, Charlotte turned her head and looked at him. The pig had been constantly at his side ever since he'd arrived home. It was almost as if she sensed something wasn't right. Max's jaw hardened at the thought. *No, something wasn't right.* He had never felt this dark before. Never felt this sense of impending doom…

He scratched Charlotte's head and the pig nudged his hand when he stopped. A little of his tension eased. "Yeah, Charlotte, I'm going to have to get my act together."

What would he do if he got the news he was done?

He had a house on the hill to build. And he had, in truth, been thinking about a family of his own. Why else had he agreed to be in that Valentine bachelor auction that his sisters had held last month? He had been called to the mission before actually being auctioned but still, he'd let them talk him into it.

Somebody who looked prettier than Charlotte

would be a plus. He wasn't sure whether he was really ready to start thinking about settling down or whether seeing his sisters so happy was just making him start to think about his future more.

He knew for certain that he wasn't ready to back away from duty yet. This gut-twisting feeling that he was having right now told him he wasn't ready to walk away. And he certainly wasn't ready to have it ripped away from him like this.

He did not want a doctor handing him his release papers.

You're still alive.

He shook himself. The thought slammed into him, interrupting his pity party.

He would take whatever tomorrow threw at him. He hadn't died in that blast with his comrades.

Thoughts of the tall horse trainer proved clearly that he had not died. He'd known she was there almost from the moment that she'd walked out onto that deck tonight. He'd shifted to find her studying him and he had hardly been able to look away from her.

Cam and Levi had noticed too, though they hadn't said anything. He'd caught both of them watching him whenever he'd tear his gaze away from Kelsey Malone. Maybe he'd go meet her tomorrow. Maybe finding out more about the beautiful horse trainer was exactly the distraction he needed right now.

CHAPTER TWO

Kelsey had just carried a child's saddle into the tack room and set it on the saddle rack when she heard the crunch of boots on gravel. She leaned around the corner, expecting to see one of the college students who worked for her arriving for work. It was Clay's morning, but instead of him she found Max Sinclair standing in the entrance of the stables. Seeing him there was as unexpected as it got.

Her pulse sped up instantly. The man had been on her mind ever since the party.

He stood in the sunlight with his hands on his lean

hips and his black T-shirt stretched tightly across his powerful chest. She tried to ignore the attraction that buzzed between them but it was not something she could ignore without effort. She forced the effort.

Her dad had been a Marine. And she'd lost him to a secret mission. She despised secret missions. Though the country needed them, and she respected the military for what they did and sacrificed for our freedoms, still Kelsey hated them.

They'd taken from her the father she had adored.

It was nothing she would ever repeat. Nothing her children would ever experience.

"Hi," she managed, trying in earnest to get resentful thoughts of her past to move back into the dark corners of her heart, where she tried to keep them suppressed. "Are you looking for Cam?"

"Yeah." He moved toward her, an almost unnoticeable limp to his right leg.

"He's not here."

"That's okay." He held out his hand. "I'm Max Sinclair. We weren't officially introduced last night."

"Kelsey Malone. It's nice to meet you." She took

his hand and swallowed hard when the rough texture of his callused hand wrapped firmly around hers. Her stomach tilted and she felt breathless.

I will not be influenced. I will not be influenced.

She pulled her hand away the moment he released it.

"I came to check out the place." He glanced around, smiling at a couple of the horses that were in the stalls instead of out in the arena. "Everything looks great."

His gaze met hers and she almost got the feeling that he was including her in that observation. *Had he come out here to check her out?*

"Thanks." She smiled. "Do you want to look around?" She felt obligated to show him around considering Cam wasn't here to do it.

"Sure."

Oh shoot. She had felt obligated but had hoped he would say no and leave. "Well, this is where we keep the horses. You probably saw most of them out in the arena."

"Yeah, I did. Bess kept the place up. There is no

telling what Cam will do for future improvements. But it's nice. Do you give riding lessons?"

"I do." She hoped he didn't ask for one. Though the idea was tempting. That was startling and worrisome to her. "Do you ride?"

"Some, though I lack my brother's love of it."

She smiled. "You're not buying a ranch in Texas?"

"That would be an affirmative."

"We better continue the tour now, I have a a class in a few minutes."

"Sure," he said. "I've actually only been out here a few times. I was never really interested in horses. But I'm changing my mind." He smiled and her heart galloped.

"Oh," she said, startled by the dimpled smile that appeared in one cheek. It was dazzling. "Well, maybe we'll get you on a horse."

He shrugged. "Maybe. But not right now."

"Oh no, not now. I noticed you were limping slightly."

"Yeah, my knee's a little stiff at the moment."

"There are ways around that if you were to really want to ride. Just let me know."

"I sure will. So who is this?" He moved toward a stall. The horse was watching him and he stroked its neck.

She strode across the distance between them and found herself smiling as she watched him with the mare. The poor horse looked a little starry-eyed.

"Well, these are the horses. This pretty lady is Sugar Cookie."

"Sweet," he said to the horse.

Her heart melted watching him. *Not good. Not good at all.*

"We have twelve horses in all. She really likes you." Kelsey laughed softly as Sugar Cookie nudged Max roughly when he stopped petting her.

"I like her too," she rubbed the opposite side of her neck, "but it looks like she only has eyes for you." The words were out before she realized what she'd said.

His lip hitched upward. "Glad someone's happy to see me."

She wasn't able to think of a comeback. "Well, uh, I'm sure you have more admirers than just Sugar Cookie," she said quickly, realizing they stood near each other. "Come this way and I'll show you where we are thinking about building a training facility." She moved toward the entrance of the stables. "Where we'll get to actually gentle them and train them." She fought to focus as she strode away from Max.

She hadn't ever felt such sudden and overwhelming attraction to someone and it was mind muddling. She needed to get a handle on it because there was no way it would ever amount to anything.

No way would she ever let it go anywhere.

Max followed Kelsey down the alley of the stable toward the entrance. The place smelled of horses, leather, and fresh hay. Obviously someone had been mucking out the stalls on a regular basis. *Was Kelsey the one doing all the mucking? From the look of the large stable, that looked like a big job. Or did the team that she talked about do it?*

His knee was killing him, so he concentrated on Kelsey and ignored the pain that radiated from his knee. Tall and slender, she walked with an energetic spring in her step that set her hips to swaying and her hair kept rhythm. He found himself enjoying following her.

Just seeing her smiling face when he'd arrived had perked up his mood. He'd been so down—really, he'd been depressed. It was hard to admit but after the loss of his two buddies and his injuries and then the unknown element of what his status would be, it had been bad.

Last night after the engagement party, he'd known he needed to try to get out of the funk he was in. And he'd decided to come meet Kelsey. She'd stood out in his mind and now he understood why. She had an energy that he was craving right now. That he needed.

On top of that, she was mesmerizing.

He shook himself. Santos and Ledger, like him, had known the risk. Their families had known the risk and they still had taken on the job. That didn't cut out the feelings that ran through him right now. He had lost men before, but somehow this time it hit too close to home. This time he'd been injured; he kept reliving the moment, trying to figure out whether he'd done something wrong. *Had he cost them their lives and him his career?*

Everything pointed to it not being his fault and he knew this but that didn't stop the guilt or the niggling worry that he'd missed something.

Kelsey suddenly paused, catching him off guard when she pivoted around. He halted and placed his full weight on his bad knee; he pitched sideways at the same time she tried to dodge slamming into him. They ended up plowing into each other. He grabbed her and fought to regain his balance on his good knee. He was mauling her and not meaning to.

She laughed. "Sorry." She tried to push away from him but he hung on to get his balance—better that than falling on his face in front of her.

At last he was steady and let her go. "My fault. I wasn't paying attention," he muttered, feeling completely inept and out of his realm. He was agile, quick, and as far from clumsy as anyone could be. Or he used to be. "I didn't mean to run you down. Are you okay?"

"I'm fine." She stepped back.

He was relieved she didn't run away. "I have to admit I enjoyed catching you." He smiled, trying to lighten the moment.

Her smile faltered and her eyes seemed to shadow. "Well, at least you're honest."

"Yeah, that I am. You can bank on that. Would you like to go out? You know, on a date, see where it goes." *Real classy, Sinclair.* He'd flubbed that, all right.

She took a deep breath to roll back on the heels of her boots. He could see her thoughts churning in those pretty eyes of hers. She was probably having to think about it so hard because he'd asked in such a clumsy way. *Or did she have a boyfriend?*

"I don't date military men," she said finally. "I'll be honest and say that I'm tempted. But, no can do. Sorry. I respect you for what you do. And I'm highly appreciative and grateful that you fight for our freedoms. But I have a policy."

Her words slammed into him. Both a challenge and a slap. Of course he should take the slap like a man and understand it. And he did understand it. This was her choice and he should respect it. Should let it go. But he didn't. "Care to elaborate on that? I'm glad to be of service but I'm curious why you have this policy."

Any other time a woman had rejected him this way, he'd let it slide off him and he'd moved on. But Kelsey's rejection hit harder. It was different to him.

She put her hand on the arena rung. One ot the horses came up and laid its head over the top of the gate. She automatically lifted her hand and rubbed the white spot between its eyes. Max followed the movement of her hand on the horse. All the more reason he wanted to know more about her "policy."

"I have my reasons. I'm…a military brat myself. And I'm not planning on raising my children that way."

"I see. Choices. I understand that. Doesn't mean I like it." They stared at each other. He watched the way she swallowed hard and those expressive eyes of hers seemed full of thoughts.

And then she bit her lip…and all he could do was think about kissing those lips and changing her mind about her policy.

Kelsey had a riot of emotions tangling through her as she looked at Max Sinclair. *This was ridiculous. Get a grip, cowgirl.*

She had to tell herself that all day long because of the way he was looking at her. And the way he was looking *to* her—this was her decision to make. It wasn't as if she hadn't seen good-looking men before. Until now, she had always been fairly immune to the special charm that the handsome cowboys in her professional life and the military men she had seen growing up seemed to have. But something about Max tossed everything to the wayside.

Her distaste for what had happened to her when she'd lost her dad growing up influenced the policy she had for not dating military men. Upholding her reputation in a man's world of sorts and the cowboy way helped her limit her encounters with cowboys. But something—something more than what she experienced before—had jumped into the fray where Max was concerned. Those eyes of his were lethal weapons. She had a feeling the only way she was going to get out of this situation was to cut the lines and cut them fast.

"I have my reasons and they won't be changed. I'm flattered, really, but I also know that you won't have any problem getting a date. None at all."

She didn't think turning her boss's brother down would harm her job; Cam Sinclair wasn't like that. But still, she'd learned in her last job that not being upfront and getting out when she knew there was trouble in the beginning would have been the best choice she could have made. So if there was going to be a problem with turning down dates from all his brothers—if she got asked by the others—then now was the time to find out. Although his other brothers, Jake and Trent, sure were also very good-looking men, being around them had not affected her the way being around Max had. Something about Max made it different, tougher to turn down and not take the date.

He studied her, a little hitch of his lips to the right. *Was that regret she saw in his eyes?*

"I guess that says it all," he said.

Her chest churned with her own regret.

He glanced around the stall and then back at her. "Then I guess I'll head out and let you get back to your business. I won't lie. There's no sense me hanging around if you feel that way."

She swallowed hard and fought the urge to take back her words. But she didn't. *Nope, she wouldn't.* Instead, she lifted her chin and cocked her head to the side. "I'm sorry. And I'm flattered. But I can't help it. I'll tell Cam you came by."

He took a step back but and held her gaze, causing all kinds of churning inside her.

"You take care of yourself, Kelsey Malone. I wish you luck with that…policy. Though I have to tell you, I'm still curious about why it's in place. But that's your business. See you later."

And then he walked away.

And oh, what a walk it was. Tall and straight.

Decisive, though she noticed he seemed to favor his left knee but seemed determined not to let it halt his steps. He was a soldier—no, he was a Marine. He was a fighting machine, that's what they were. *Semper Fi*...honor, courage, and commitment—she knew their motto well. Her father had also.

No matter what she was feeling, no matter the regret that washed through her as she watched him disappear into the sunlight, Max Sinclair was off-limits.

Max got in his truck and forced himself not to glance back at the stable. It was done; he would honor her decision. Everybody was entitled to their opinion. He didn't know what her reasons were, but it wasn't his business to try to change them. He didn't like it, though. Felt downright insulted. And that was wrong; like he said, he didn't know her reasons. But as he drove back into Windswept Bay, the pretty blue water glistening out his window, his thoughts churned and he could not let it go.

He drove up to the beachside bungalow that housed his brother Jake's dive shop. The low-slung building had a host of beach paraphernalia outside, showing what to expect inside. Surfboards, oxygen tanks, nets, and wet suits hung from a rack. It was an unassuming place that stayed really busy.

Jake loved diving. Loved sometimes looking for treasure off the coast if something interested him. His brother didn't seem to have a care in the world other than living life to the fullest. Max might need a few pointers on that if he ended up being booted from service.

He and Jake had been through a lot together. They'd lost both their parents when they were young and had not only grieved, but thanked goodness for their parents' friendship with Sam and Violet Sinclair and having named them godparents. That had at least relieved him and Jake on what was going to happen to them. But Violet and Sam had taken it a step further and later had adopted them, bringing them fully into the family and giving them their full protection in the courts. But despite that Jake was his blood brother,

Max hadn't been able to talk about his top-secret missions. And that made it hard on them sometimes.

All of his brothers understood about his career but still, it put distance between them all and right now Max felt isolated.

He walked into the shop. Several people milled around, checking out different areas of the shop. In the retail area, a lady and her son were checking out the T-shirts. Two divers checked out the diving gear. He continued on to the shop and passed through the bait area, where Jake sold all kinds of fishing tackle and bait to all the fishermen. He moved on into the actual shop at the back and then walked out into the back deck where all the boats were docked. The skies were clear and the water smooth. He spotted Jake on the deck of the dive boat, preparing it for the next dive. Max strode out onto the dock.

Jake spotted him and lifted his hand. "Hey bro, you coming on? Coming for a dive?"

Max paused at the boat and squinted in the sun despite his aviators. "Not today. But it looks like you're getting ready."

"Yeah, gotta nice size group coming on in about thirty minutes. We're going out to the reef. You sure you don't want to come? I can always use an extra dive master. You know that's an open-ended invitation. Anytime you decide to become a civilian, I have a job offer for you."

Max didn't even grin. He just acknowledged Jake's words. It was a discussion they had often.

"You on for maybe going out when you get back tonight? I'm feeling restless. I don't think I can spend another night with Charlotte. We're kind of getting bored with each other since I've been back."

Jake laughed. "I can understand. That's some piggy you've got there but I can see she might not be the best of company. You know me—I'm always ready."

"You know the place." He called out the local pool hall. "I can pick you up or I can meet you there."

Jake grinned. "I'll meet you there."

"Good. I'm looking to win a bet." He hitched a brow.

Jake hooted. "My recollection is that the last time

we played pool that I walked away with a pocket full of quarters."

They only played for quarters. But they took it seriously and they had played all night. "Just because you were a sore loser and wouldn't stop till you were ahead. We'll put a quarter limit and a time limit on it tonight. At midnight sharp—any competition we have going will be over. Period."

"Whatever you say, little brother. I've been needing some change anyway. You've been home a week now. Do you expect to go on a mission anytime soon?"

Max shrugged. "You know how it goes—you never know. They call, I go." No need to say that he wasn't going till he got the verdict on his knee…and his hearing.

He hid his limp pretty good, he thought, but according to doctors, he needed to wait several months before surgery to repair it. Until then, he had to be careful not to damage it worse. Crutches would be good but not necessary if he were careful. The swelling of the initial injury needed to go down and he was doing rehab at home to help the muscles strengthen.

When could he go on another mission…it was up in the air right now. But the reality was if his hearing test results came back and didn't meet standards, he was out. It wouldn't matter whether his knee recovered fully or not.

If anyone realized he had a limp, they wouldn't know how serious his problems were. But Max did. He thought about it constantly. He pushed the thoughts away and finished his sentence. "And if they don't call, I stay till they do."

"Yeah—gotcha."

"You're not dating anybody?" he asked Jake, trying to change the subject.

Jake rolled up lines. He laughed and squinted at Max. "I date. I just don't, you know, linger long. Not in me. Not right now."

That was Jake. Jake never lingered. He played the field as if he were throwing fast pitches.

"All right, I was just curious. You're not thinking about your future—home and hearth and family?"

Jake paused. "Hey, you getting all sentimental on

me? I know our sisters have all found marital bliss and all that. Looks like Levi and Cam have too but I'm not ready for that. I'm not exactly what you'd call marriage material." He shrugged. "I'm just not ready."

Max had never really pushed, mostly because he wasn't ready either. But looking at Jake now, something gleamed in his eyes that Max had never noticed before. Maybe it was because he hadn't wanted to.

Maybe he and Jake were both fighting the tides…torn about what they really wanted out of life at this time of their lives. Or maybe it was just Max.

CHAPTER THREE

The next day, Kelsey was finishing up the afternoon riding lessons. She had been busy all day. Plenty of people had come out to ride and she had lessons for three now in her after-school group. Kevin, Max Sinclair's brother Levi's fiancée Jessica's little boy, was the cutest thing. He had gone to school and proclaimed to his classroom that he was having riding lessons. Two of his classmates called and signed up for classes. So now it wasn't just Kevin in the afternoon but his two friends Alan and Ben also. They kept her laughing during the lessons and she was enjoying herself immensely.

Their parents had asked her whether she could handle more and she'd told them maybe a couple. But she didn't want the class too big. It would be a little like herding cats if she let too many that age on horses at one time. She'd keep it small.

Hank, one of the guys who worked for her, was cleaning the stalls so she headed inside the house, where she was slowly beginning to settle in. Cam had given her the house to live in while she was managing the place. He would stay at the resort when he was here visiting or at his parents' until he figured out what he was going to do on the place. He and Lana, his fiancée, had talked about building a home on the property that overlooked the ocean. So for now she was very grateful that she had the house and that she felt safe and comfortable there. That had never been the case at her other job.

At her former job, she had lived on the property and it had been a disaster in the end, especially when it was clear that keeping her boss outside of boundary lines turned out to be a really hard thing to do. It turned out it also was a really hard thing to stop the rumors…*untrue* rumors…when they started. So she had had to really consider the situation when Cam had told her that she would be in the house. He understood some of her troubles with her last job. Being in the horse industry, it had been hard not to have heard the rumors. He'd hired her anyway and he'd suspected she might have a hard time with the proposition. He'd made it very clear that it was her choice but that she had nothing to fear from him. She was grateful for that.

Max had been on her mind since he'd been here the day before. The handsome Marine would not go away. No matter how many times she pushed him from her thoughts, he'd persisted and continually shown back up. *It was ridiculous and it was only asking for trouble*, she told herself as she poured herself a glass of tea. She took it outside onto the back porch. Sitting there gave her a little bit of privacy from the arena and stables on the front of the house but it also gave her a small view of the ocean. She enjoyed sitting here in the evenings and quietly reading over the books and the numbers and doing her paperwork. She had quickly grown to love it and also her life here on the ocean.

Today, she was making a grocery list, but her mind kept wandering to Max instead of the needed items she was trying to think of and write down.

She pushed Max from her thoughts, telling herself that she was barking up a dangerous tree…and an unwanted one. But maybe it didn't hurt to at least think about the guy. She was, after all, single, unattached, and available. But she wasn't.

Not to a military man. *Especially someone in Special Ops.*

Salad. She needed salad, tomatoes, ranch dressing—she loved ranch dressing. She loved it with everything: carrots, chicken strips, French fries… *Does Max Sinclair like ranch dressing?*

Stop thinking about the man!

It didn't matter whether he liked it or not; the man was off-limits.

She frowned and tossed her pen on the table. She stared at the ocean as so many thoughts of the time spent after learning her dad had been killed in action spun through her.

It wasn't Max's fault that she couldn't forget what she'd sacrificed for her country. But that didn't matter. Turning away, she headed inside. It was time to go to town and get her groceries. It was time to stop thinking about Max.

She'd eaten all of her meals alone since coming to town, except for the night she'd gone to the engagement party. Maybe it was time to start thinking about getting out more. But right now, she was getting out by going to the grocery store.

Max was getting crosstown to play pool with Jake again tonight. They played the night before and had such a good time they decided to play again tonight. It had helped getting out of the house and it would help him once again to not let his brain obsess over the pretty girl training horses at his brother's business. *Kelsey Malone was off-limits, period.*

He was telling himself that as he drove to the parking lot and parked in front of the pool hall. He saw that he'd missed a call from Jake. He hadn't heard it ring so he checked and saw the sound was turned down. He listened to the message.

"Hey bro, sorry to do this to you but I'm not going to make it tonight. You'll have to find someone else to take money from instead of me. Sorry this is last minute but couldn't be helped. Had a boat break down and had to go pick everyone up. Talk to you later."

He had no desire to go inside and find strangers to play pool with. Instead, he cranked his truck and pulled out of the parking lot. Feeling restless and more tempted than he wanted to admit, he had to fight not to turn his truck in the direction of the stables. He forced himself to turn the opposite direction. Maybe he'd go see his folks…too many questions might meet him there, though, so instead he'd go home. He stopped at the red light on the corner, thoughts of Kelsey on his mind again. He tapped his fingers on the steering wheel to the beat of the music as he stared across the street to the grocery store parking lot. He guessed he could go to the store.

Then, suddenly, he saw Kelsey. It took a second to realize that the woman striding at a determined pace across the parking lot was Kelsey. It was as if she'd walked out of his head and onto the pavement. She did not look happy. He concentrated; yes, she looked upset. And then he saw the man stalking twenty paces behind her. He picked up his pace as Max stared. He wore a white button-up shirt, jeans, boots, and a Stetson. Just before she reached her truck, he reached her. He talked to her and she said something over her shoulder as he grabbed her arm.

"What the—" Max sat up straight as the man yelled something at Kelsey and she began trying to pull her arm out of his grasp. The light turned green and he stomped the gas. He would have run the light if he'd needed to. He shot across the intersection and into the parking lot, screeching tires as he turned the corner, and drove straight at the man. Kelsey was struggling with the man as Max slammed on his brakes. He bailed out of the truck just as Kelsey broke free from the man's grip and fell to the ground. The man bent over her. Max did not hesitate as he blasted out of the truck. Stepping on his bad knee without care, a sharp, jagged pain ripped through him. He grunted; his knee buckled but he stayed upright as he shot across the few feet between him and the man. Max tackled him and they both flew to the ground. Max was seeing red as he quickly flipped the man to his back and yanked his arm back and up, making it so the man couldn't move. He could yell, though, and was doing plenty of that.

"Get off me. Let me go."

Max ignored him. "Kelsey, you okay?" He watched as she scrambled up from the ground and rubbed her arm.

She looked dazed as she stared from him to her assailant. "I, I'm fine. He just, he just grabbed me."

"Call 911."

She just stared at the man, who yelled threats at her.

"Kelsey, look at me. Are you okay?" he asked again, wanting to reach out to her. "Are you sure you're not hurt?"

"I didn't hurt her," the man growled.

"Stop struggling and shut your mouth. You're lucky I took it easy on you. Kelsey, answer me—are you okay?" His heart thundered as he pulled his phone from his pocket and punched Levi's number in with his thumb. He punched his knee into the man's kidney harder when he squirmed. Max never took his gaze off Kelsey and finally she nodded her head.

"Sorry. I'm just…shaken up."

Levi answered the call. "Hey, Max—"

"Levi, I need you at the grocery store on Main. A man attacked Kelsey in the parking lot. And I've got him but you'll need to get here."

"I'm not far. I'm on my way."

Max rammed the phone back into his shirt pocket.

"You'll hear from my lawyer," the man threatened.

"You're really going to threaten that? I saw you grab her. I saw you follow her out of the store." Sirens sounded in the distance.

"Maybe this is a bad idea," Kelsey said.

"Yeah, it's a bad idea," the man growled. "She won't press charges."

Max stared at Kelsey. "Do you know this guy?"

She nodded. "He's Alton Harrison, my ex-boss."

CHAPTER FOUR

Levi stood Harrison up, having arrived and directed Max to let him take over.

Max stood to the side and struggled to understand what was going on. Kelsey's *ex-boss? What was that all about?*

"Are you going to press charges, Kelsey?" Levi asked.

To Max's surprise, she shook her head. "No. I just want him to go away and leave me alone. Go back to your wife and your business. There is nothing for you here, Harrison," she told the guy, staring at him with hard eyes.

Max glared at her. "It's none of my business but it seems to me if the guy is harassing you that you need to press charges so he'll leave you alone. He can't just do this and get away with it."

"You don't understand, Max."

"No, I don't."

Levi let the man go. "You understand that she could press charges. Come with me and hand over your driver's license. I'm writing you a warning for disturbing the peace. And if you come back in my jurisdiction and cause trouble again, I'll book you. Got it?"

"I'll have my lawyer sue every one of you," Harrison snarled.

Max stepped closer, the pain in his knee almost unbearable. "You better get in your truck and get out of here while you can. I won't go as easy on you next time." He should have broken the piece of dirt's arm. He looked at Kelsey. "You're sure you're not pressing charges?"

She shook her head. "I'm sure. I just want this to

go away."

It probably wasn't that easy, he wanted to tell her, but kept his mouth zipped so he wouldn't say more than he should. He leaned against his truck and waved a hand at Levi. "Get him out of here." He said nothing to Kelsey.

She wrapped her arms together and could not look at him as they waited for Levi to get his info. Then, after another warning and the man spouting off more threats, they watched him storm to his truck and drive away.

Max could feel steam billowing out of his ears, he was so furious. Kelsey had been attacked and she'd backed down. It was not what he'd expected.

Levi stuffed his hands on his hips and watched the man go and then turned back to Kelsey. "He may be back. Call if you need help. It was your call but I don't like it. I better get back. You okay, Max?"

Max was pretty sure his brother could see the steam cloud hovering around him. "I'm not going to lie, I'm pretty hot. But I'm fine. Thanks for coming."

"We'll talk later." Levi got into his patrol vehicle

and drove away.

Max pushed away from his truck and his knee buckled. He grabbed the truck bed to steady himself.

"You're hurt," Kelsey gasped and rushed to him.

"I'm fine," he gritted between teeth.

"No, you're not. Here—put your arm over my shoulders and let's get you in the truck. Can you drive?"

"I can drive." He hated the focus on him now but he slipped his arm over her shoulder and let her help him get to the driver's seat. She wrapped her arm around his waist and helped him.

"I am so sorry," she said.

He sank onto the seat and supported his knee as he pulled his throbbing leg into the truck. "Care to get in and explain to me what that was all about?"

She nodded and then hurried to the passenger side and climbed in. He closed his door and cranked the truck, letting the air conditioning cool the interior. Nothing could cool his temper, but he kept his voice even and his opinion shut down. For now.

"He was my boss. I lived on his property and he

thought, obviously because I lived there and I worked for him, that I was his. At first, I just tried to do my job and ignore the disturbing signals I was getting from him. I ignored his suggestive comments and made sure to avoid being alone with him or moved out of range of his hands…as best that I could. He's married but that hadn't seemed to matter to him. I finally came right out and told him I was there to do a job: train his horses. I thought he would back down. Max, I am good at what I do. I'd hoped that I had the job based on that. But he had other ideas and started showing up at the house. It's embarrassing." She looked away. "I didn't let him in."

Max's jaw tightened. He wanted the man back here so he could teach him a lesson on how to treat a lady. He could tell Kelsey was disgusted by the whole idea but why hadn't she pressed charges? It didn't make sense. "Go on."

"Rumors started that we were an item. At the shows, I realized what people were thinking and it disgusted and embarrassed me. When I confronted him about it, he said he would put a stop to them. And like a naïve child, I believed him. And then he showed up one night and let himself into the house with his own key."

"Did he attack you?"

"No. I locked the bedroom door and he finally left. I quit the next morning and then the rumors really did start. Thanks to your brother, here I am and I have a job. I thought it was over. Obviously I was wrong. But I have just been drug through the mud already. I can't go through that again. That's why I didn't press charges."

"Maybe but if you want this to stop, you need to take him to court," he urged, gripping the steering wheel so hard his knuckles were white.

She blinked hard; he saw tears in her eyes and then down her cheeks. She wiped them away. "You're hurt and it's my fault. I am so sorry. This is such a mess."

"I was already hurt. I just wasn't telling anyone. I was going to. It's just overstressed. I probably need to go home and ice it down for a while."

"I'll go with you and make the ice pack for you.

I'm not ready to go home."

He nodded. "Then buckle up. This is a little bit of a drive."

Kelsey could not believe that because of her Max was hurt. She couldn't believe that her ex-boss had followed her here. She thought she was over that nightmare. And she could tell that Max and Levi both were not happy about her decision. But they didn't understand.

They traveled in silence for several miles. She wanted to ask Max about his knee but she didn't want him to ask her more about her ex-boss.

Finally he said, "He didn't force himself on you, did he?"

She stiffened as she remembered the night he tried. "No, he tried but I got away from him and locked myself in the bedroom and threatened to call the cops."

"Something tells me you're not telling the whole story. And I guess I know it's not any of my business. I guess you can do what you want but it doesn't make sense to me."

"Can we talk about something else?" She could see tension lines in his forehead and knew his leg was hurting him pretty badly. "Are we almost there? You really need some ice and you probably need to see a doctor."

"I'm fine. And we're here." He pulled into a dirt road that was short with a locked gate. He pulled a key off the console and handed it to her. "Do you mind unlocking it?"

She took the key; their fingers brushed and she felt a tingle of awareness. She curled her fingers around the key. She didn't need to feel the thrill running through her. "I'll be right back."

She jumped out of the truck as if wildfire were chasing her and strode over to the gate. She had it unlocked quickly and then slung the gate open and waited as he drove through.

"No need to relock it. I'll be taking you home in a little while," he called out the window.

Why did he have a gate like this and not a remote gate?

She climbed back into the truck and he drove around the bend. Immediately the beach glistened before them. It was a beautiful spot. His own private oasis.

The sun was almost gone but still, even in the low light it was gorgeous. "It's beautiful. I'm sure in daylight it's amazing."

"I found the spot years ago and grabbed the land immediately. I haven't had time to make all my improvements but it gives me something to do when I'm home. I like the seclusion of it."

He pulled to a halt in front of a small faded blue house, a tiny place. It was a beachside hut, really. On one side was a covered area with a grill and chairs. Outdoor lights were on, illuminating the colorful chairs. It was his own little paradise. The perfect place to get away…and for a single guy, it probably worked perfectly.

She climbed out of the truck. The moment her foot touched the sand, a horrible screeching erupted and a short, fat pig charged from the shadows, straight at her.

"Does it bite?" She looked back to find Max

laughing.

"No, it doesn't. Charlotte is just full of hot air. She's my watch pig."

"Your what?" she asked as the pig reached her, skidded to a halt and looked up at her with beady eyes.

"Charlotte is a bit territorial, so she just needs to get used to you. Be nice, Charlotte," he said in a firm voice. Immediately, the pig looked up, trying to see him over the edge of the seat. Max leaned over toward Kelsey so that Charlotte could see him. Immediately, the squiggly pig's tail began to wag.

Kelsey laughed; it was so absurd. "Is she going to bite my hand if I try to pet her?"

"No, she will adore you if you scratch her ears."

"I am truly surprised." She shot him a smile before she reached down to scratch Charlotte's ears. The pig practically smiled as it stretched to keep contact with Kelsey's fingertips. "Well, you're cute, I'll give you that. But I need to go help the man in your life out of the truck."

Charlotte trotted beside her as she rounded the front of the truck. Max had the door opened and was already standing, with his hands on the door.

"You've made a friend for life. She'll be your buddy now."

"That's good to know." She smiled at him. "Now, let's get you inside. Then you'll have to tell me how you came to own a pig. And don't be all Mr. Macho because I know you're in pain."

"I'm not in too much pain to know that when a certain beautiful horse trainer offers to step into my arms I should let her."

She laughed as he placed his arm over her shoulders and she wrapped her arm around his waist.

"Ready?"

"Anytime."

He was looking at her and she caught her breath as she looked up at him and had the overwhelming wish to kiss him. *Not what she needed to be thinking about.*

"Let's go."

He gave a low, sexy chuckle as they started toward the house. It almost covered up the grunt she heard escape him as he took the first step.

Charlotte trotted beside them, very curious about

what they were doing. She reached the door first and nudged it with her nose.

"I take it she's used to opening the door sometimes?"

"Yes, though not often. She knows that sometimes it doesn't latch all the way and she can sneak inside."

He pulled a key from his pocket and unlocked it. "You can go lay back down, Charlotte," he told her as they maneuvered through the door. The pig snorted and trotted away obediently.

"You not only have a pig but a trained pig."

"Yup. She's a watch pig and takes her job seriously. She was a quick learner."

"I'm amazed."

He switched on a light and the room lit up. It was colorful and the furniture was plain but unique. It looked handmade.

"I like this room."

"Thanks. I try."

She helped him to the couch and he eased down onto it. "I'll get the ice. Do you have some painkillers?"

"Cabinet by the refrigerator."

She headed into the small adjoining kitchen separated from the living space by a bar and chairs. "So how did you get Charlotte?" She opened the freezer. An assortment of ice packs were chilling inside. "Goodness, you're prepared."

"Yeah, in my line of work, you never know how many ice packs you'll need."

She frowned at the reminder that he probably often came home from a mission hurting. No telling how far he had to sometimes hike or climb to reach whatever mission he was on. Or how often he was hurt.

"I got her as a baby. I'd read they were good guards and if need be, she can scrounge for herself. There are plenty of roots and bugs out here for her to survive on if she had to."

She walked back into the room and handed him the ibuprofen and a glass of water. She then grabbed the ice pack and handed it to him.

He put it on his knee and then leaned his head back on the colorful cushion. "Thank you," he said.

"That was much needed."

She sank into the edge of the chair opposite the couch. He had his eyes closed and she found herself studying him. She looked away. *Better that than studying his chiseled features.* Instead, she studied the room.

"Are you nervous?"

She looked over to find him watching her. She leaned back on the cushion, trying to relax. "No. Why would I be?"

His lip hitched into that smile of his and there was that dimple that showed up sometimes.

"That's right. Why would you be? Relax. You're safe with me."

She wondered how much pain he was in. He wasn't showing it but she felt as if it was a lot and it was her fault.

"I'm just processing everything. I know you can't say anything about your mission or anything but obviously you're hurt fairly significantly. Are you worried about that?"

His face shadowed. "It could alter my status.

Could alter the trajectory of my life. And I haven't told anyone that."

For military men dedicated to their careers, driven to serve and sacrifice like him—like her father—this was a really hard situation for him and she knew it. Could hear it in his voice and see it in the look in his serious eyes. The fact that he had not told any of his family about his situation was also telling. Denial was a hard mistress.

"When will you know?"

He tensed. "I have a doctor's appointment next week for evaluation. I'll know more after that."

Guilt shrouded her. "I am so sorry. Today didn't help at all…it could have undone any progress you'd made." She rubbed her neck as she tensed up. *What if his knee had been healing and then because he had helped her, it had been damaged worse? What if they released him from service and it was her fault?*

His eyes were grave. "I'd do it again to stop that jerk from hurting you."

That was the sweetest thing anyone had ever said to her. How selfless he was.

"I wish you'd press charges on him. I don't have a good feeling about this and feel like you're going to be in danger."

She groaned. "So now that doesn't make me feel better."

"Maybe not, but it's the truth."

"I don't want to be dragged through the mud again. I want to live here on Windswept Bay and feel good about my life again."

"But you never did anything wrong. He did. And you're letting him off the hook."

They stared at each other…and she wasn't exactly sure what to say.

CHAPTER FIVE

Max could not keep his eyes off Kelsey. He was trying not to stare but wasn't winning. The pain in his knee distracted him a little bit. But, still, something about her got to him. And he could not get her situation off his mind.

"So you're liking working for Cam and you aren't into military men and you have an ex-boss stalker. What else is there for me to know about Kelsey Malone?" He gave a slight grin, hoping to ease the presentation of his words. But he wanted to know about her. And in truth, those three things were all he knew about her. He knew now why she was working for Cam and what had happened to her at her last job. Still, none of that explained why she wouldn't date a military man.

She laughed. "That is not the story of my life. There is more; it just seems that right now that's it. I think you and I have something in common right now, though." She looked at him with a slight grin.

He really liked that grin. But the truth was he liked everything about her. "Yeah?" he said, unable to keep the flirt out of his voice. "And what would that be?"

"We're both in transition. I'm transitioning from fear, junk from the other job. And you're transitioning from something you love, to accepting something that is going to happen inevitably one way or the other. Can you deal with that? Not everyone can."

She had looked into him and saw exactly what was going on in his head. He knew it was like a pro quarterback in a football game—they could only go so far. Whether they loved it or not, there was always someone younger, faster, and ready to move up the ranks and take their place. And eventually it would happen. The quarterback could then decide to hang around too long or retire, still on the top of his game. He wasn't judging anybody; he wouldn't do that. But he did admire the ones who moved on while they were still on top rather than the ones who just couldn't let it go and kept coming back until it was a must and they tarnished their record. They got to him—got him in the gut. *Who was he going to be?*

"You got it. I am dealing with that right now. I don't want to be the quarterback who can't quit."

"Yeah, I get that. I know what you're talking about. It's hard but the reality is that your knee might be weak when this is over and it's hard to know. Your team relies on each person. What are you going to do if your weakened knee blows when you're trying to carry out a wounded member…when your team needs you to save a life?"

"Is that what happened?"

She looked at him sharp, alert. She swallowed hard. "Yes, actually. My dad. He didn't know when to get out. He didn't want to get out and it didn't matter that he had a wife and daughter to come home who needed him. All that mattered was one more trip. Just one more. In the end, he didn't come home. And neither did a couple of guys in his platoon. It was rough. And now you know all my reasoning behind my policy."

He was stunned. And his heart hurt for her because he could see in the paleness of her face and the pain in her eyes that it mattered to her. It might not have mattered in the end to her dad—but it had marked her for life.

And he wasn't sure how to help her. "I'm sorry about your dad. That's really tough."

"Thanks. I've put it behind me, but won't go there in my future."

"I understand and am sorry for me." He smiled gently at her and the tension in her eased. "So, what if we have something to eat? I know you have your policy but we have to eat...aren't you hungry? I have burgers and can grill some up." It was worth a shot— he wasn't ready for her to leave and they had to eat. You couldn't blame a guy for trying.

"You are in no shape to be cooking. I think I better

go home. Honestly, I just don't know about this attraction zipping between us. It can't go anywhere."

Wow. She was blunt and honest. And he liked it. He liked it a lot.

One thing was for certain: you knew where you stood where Kelsey was concerned. Obviously her ex-boss had been dimwitted or had just ignored her non-interest. Unless she'd been a little more diplomatic when it came to a boss. Still, as far as Max was concerned, the guy had no ground to stand on for what he'd done.

She stood and Max felt a bit desperate to keep her here longer.

"So, the knee is feeling better and it's time to take the ice pack off. I'm putting burgers on the grill and I have some mighty comfortable chairs out there. There's a gorgeous moon out...no strings attached. Just a shared meal." He sounded desperate but he didn't want to be alone tonight—for the evening. Not again. Didn't want to think about his mission and didn't want to think about his future. He just wanted to sit on the beach with a pretty woman and listen to the waves and watch the moon sparkle on the water.

But he didn't want just any woman. He wanted Kelsey Malone.

Kelsey was so tempted. She was so tempted, it was unbelievable and yet… "I really need to go home."

He looked disappointed and that hit her hard in the chest.

"Okay." He started to get up. "I'll take you home then."

She hesitated. "Okay." Kelsey watched Max stand. He grimaced slightly and she knew he was hiding the pain from her when he tried to cover it up with a grin. He was a Marine; of course he would try to hide it. He was probably trained to handle pain. Which led her to know that whatever was going on behind that kneecap of his was really bad. *Really bad.*

Guilt hit her. "Wait. What are you going to eat if you take me home?"

He shrugged. "I'll come back and fix the burgers just like I planned but without the good company." His brows knit in the most provocative way over his blue eyes. Her insides tumbled a bit.

The man was injured because of her and he was going to have to stand on his injured knee and fix his own meal. She needed to knock her forehead against a wall for a minute. She was being selfish because she was scared of him. Yes, no denying it.

She wanted to go home and take the easy way out…and that was completely wrong.

"Okay, here's the deal. I'll agree to stay as long as you sit and let me do the grilling and the rest of the meal."

He started to speak and she knew he was about to say no. She held up her hand. "No—that's the way I'll agree to stay. The only way I'll stay. You are hurt because you helped me, so it's only right I fix you something to eat. I know how to grill burgers. As a matter of fact, I'm really good at grilling burgers. I learned it from my granddaddy. So if you want my special burgers and if you want my company for the evening, then you agree to sit in one of those comfy chairs you told me about while I fix you dinner."

He got the sexiest look on his face as a smile spread wide. *There was that dimple again.* That dimple didn't always show up—it was as if it only came out on special occasions. Special moments…and oh boy, was it out right now.

She could slap herself. *She was in so much trouble.*

"If that's the terms, then I guess I'm heading out there to sit down right now."

She laughed, walked over and put her arm around his waist to assist him. Her insides trembled as she did so. He paused and looked at her.

She groaned silently and tried not to think about the fact that they were practically embracing. "Okay," she managed, giving herself a kick in the pants. "Put your arm around me and let's go. I'll get you outside and in a chair and then I'll get a tray and bring all the fixings out and get the burgers started."

His arm slid over and she was so very aware of the side of her body pressed against the side of his body and of that arm wrapped over her shoulders. Her heart raced and butterflies fluttered everywhere possible—

from the tips of her toes to the roots of her hair. She probably had butterflies burst from the tips of her hair and flying around her head right now.

The emotions she felt were crazy and amazing.

"Um, cookie sheet and stuff…I mean, seasonings."

He smiled. "Cookie sheets are in that tall cabinet. The hamburger is in a bowl in the refrigerator. I haven't spiced it up yet, so you can have at it. Spices are in the cabinet above the stove and the buns are in the pantry, along with an assortment of chips. I like spicy ranch flavor."

She sighed. *The man was just so irresistible…and he had the most wonderful voice—* She yanked her resolve up by the collar and cleared her throat. "Sounds like you've got it all covered. Let's go on out the door."

So she could concentrate and get her head on straight. Good grief!

Thankfully, it didn't take too long to cross the small room and move to the chairs. The sound of the surf was gentle from this distance and the moon looked like a big light hovering on the horizon. It was dazzling, shooting a golden trail endless miles across the dark water straight to them.

"You were right—that is irresistible and unmissable."

"Told you. I'm glad you stayed."

She was too. After she helped him into his chair, she went back inside. Everything was where he had told her it would be. His kitchen was so organized, it was obvious that the man was in the military: everything had a place and it was perfectly in line. She smiled. They were so different on that end. She always had to hunt for things…he'd die looking for spices because some were in one cabinet and others were…elsewhere. Whatever cabinet it was sitting by when she cleaned off the counter.

She gathered everything together and went back outside and set the loaded tray on the table. Charlotte had come to sit on her haunches at Max's feet. The pig adored him, it was clear.

Charlotte turned her head and watched Kelsey as if very curious about everything Kelsey did. It was almost as though she were making a claim on Max and guarding him from Kelsey.

She put the coals in the pit and reached for starter fluid and then the lighter that he had on the rack beside the pit. Within moments, the coals were flaming.

"You did that like a pro."

She turned and found Max watching her with a small grin.

"Ha, so you didn't believe me. Grilling is not just for men."

He chuckled. "I'm perfectly comfortable with that."

She chuckled. "Good to know your manliness isn't threatened by it."

"Not at all. I'm looking forward to this."

He had a sink in the rack next to the grill and she assumed it acted as a grilling station and also a fish cleaning station. She turned the water on and then prepared the patties while the coals heated up. Once she'd washed her hands, she set the tray of patties beside the grill and then pulled out the cutting board and went to work slicing tomatoes.

"You have a nice setup out here."

"Thanks. It works for me. I very seldom cook in the kitchen."

Everything was ready so she placed the patties on the grill and put the top on. "I'll go get drinks now. I saw you have an assortment of things in your refrigerator. What can I get you?"

"I'll actually have a bottle of water, if you don't mind. Have whatever you want."

She went inside and grabbed plates and the chips and two waters. Charlotte trotted over to her as she set the chips on the table. "I still can't believe you have a pig. She's sweet, though, and loves you dearly, it's clear."

"Yes, she does. But I can tell you that right now she loves you more."

Kelsey's brows knitted. "Me?"

He nodded. "You have the chips. That pig loves chips like a cat loves catnip. I'm surprised when she spotted that package she didn't ram you in the knees and tackle you for them."

She laughed. "Seriously?"

"Oh, I'm serious. We don't kid about potato chips around here. She will take them any way she can get them and in any flavor. She is not a picky pig."

She still could not get over the fact that he had a pig for a pet but it was growing on her. She reached down and scratched Charlotte's pink forehead. Charlotte's curly tail wagged so fast her rump shook. It was hilarious and Kelsey laughed. "Oh, she likes this too."

He shook his head. "Yes, she does."

"So should I give her a chip?"

"That would probably be a good idea because in a minute she's going to stop being nice and try to knock over the table to get them."

Kelsey grimaced. "Then I'll hand her one."

"Make that two or three. And would you mind tossing me a bag?"

"Sure." She grabbed a bag of the ranch and handed them across to him, along with the water.

"Thanks. I am addicted to them, too. I'm trying to limit them, though, because I'm not getting my exercise like I need to and I'm afraid I'll put on pounds." He grinned.

"You and I both know you don't have any worries about pounds. With the shape you are in, your metabolism is probably fired up at twenty times of that of a normal person like me. You're burning calories just sitting there."

That made him smile. "Yeah, but if my knee doesn't get fixed soon it's going to slow down."

"Well, for tonight enjoy your chips. Here, I'll actually take some too." She reached into the bag and grabbed a handful. He laughed and bit down on one as they smiled at each other.

And so the rest of the evening went. She got the burgers off the grill and fixed their burgers. She passed a plate to Max before she sat down in a comfortable chair next to him and they ate and listened to the surf.

It was so nice. She had been eating most of her meals alone and realized earlier that afternoon she'd been thinking she needed to get out more because she was tired of eating alone.

She'd had no idea at that moment that tonight she'd be eating with Max.

He had his leg propped up on a stool and noticed him grimace a few times. She suspected his leg was starting to throb and hurt again. She wanted to ask whether he was going to take a painkiller but he was an adult and she wasn't his keeper.

She had to remind herself of that.

He was an adult and would take it if he wanted it.

"You really intrigued me," he said, startling her from her thoughts.

"Well, I don't exactly understand why. I have loads of baggage, as you found out tonight, but other than that, I'm just a normal woman."

"Um, no. I don't think so. You run deep. And…I'll be honest, I don't like your policy at all. I can tell you, Kelsey Malone, this isn't the only meal I want to share with you. I'd like to take you to dinner. A nice place, maybe to Calypso's. Or to the beachside restaurant at the resort. My sisters have really done an amazing job renovating the resort and that new dining spot, I hear, is really fantastic. I've been too busy to go and I haven't had anyone to invite. But I would love to take you to a nice meal and sit down and spend some more time with you without the pig around."

He was serious she could tell. She liked that he was as blunt as she was. He was getting more and more irresistible with every passing moment.

He took a bite of his burger and chewed, watching her reaction to what he'd said.

She took another bite and then a drink of her water. Finally, she smiled. "You don't take no for an answer, do you?"

"No, not when I'm on a mission. I know I'm supposed to accept it, but I can't help it. I'd say I want to take you skydiving or hiking or somewhere a little more adventurous than just a meal but I'm a little bit out of sorts at the moment and it's not a possibility. So I'm being realistic on that part."

She laughed. "You're impossible. You drive a hard bargain but I'm just as stubborn as you are and the answer is no. I've fixed you this meal and shared this lovely evening to repay you for saving me this afternoon but that's it. Now you're going to take me home and then come home and get in your bed and rest. If you stay off it for a few days maybe, hopefully, when you get to that doctor next week, you'll get a good report. You'll get to keep doing what you love to do for a little longer and as far as I'm concerned, if that's what you want, that's not something that I can be a part of. Not even just for a date. And you need to understand that and accept it."

He frowned and she continued…she had to, maybe to reaffirm her stance to herself.

"Yes, I am tempted, very tempted. I'm more tempted than I've ever been in my life to make an exception." Maybe she shouldn't have said *that*. "I'm honest but no, it can't happen. So…" She rose and set her empty plate on the table. She needed to go home and she needed to go home now. Because hanging out with him was just going to make it worse

CHAPTER SIX

A few days later, Kelsey was invited to Windswept Bay Resort for a girl's night out with Lana, Jessica, and the Sinclair sisters. They were having a fun night and she had been invited by Lana and Jessica to come because everyone knew she hadn't had time to make friends in town.

She was enjoying getting to know people but so far most of the people she'd met at the stables were tourists. She was so grateful for the invitation. It was going to be great to hang out with women…friends. She had been missing hanging out with women her own age.

She walked into the beautiful lobby of the resort with much anticipation. Lana had told her she would pick her up but Lana was teaching school and she didn't want to make her drive all the way out to the stables. Cam was back in Texas at his ranch while Lana finished out her last couple of months teaching before they married. She hadn't wanted to have the wedding until she could marry and move with him back to Texas. It was actually working out so that Kelsey was getting to know Lana and Jessica, and now she would spend more time with Max's sisters.

They waved as she walked past the reception area into the wide-open lobby of the beautiful resort with the winding staircase. Lana and Shar, one of the Sinclair triplets, stood at the base of the staircase. And as she approached, she saw Cali, the oldest Sinclair sister, and Jillian, a second triplet, coming down the stairs from the second floor. Jillian was pregnant and had a small baby bump beneath her sun dress. She looked completely radiant.

She thought the resort offices were housed up

there but she wasn't certain. Lana came toward her and hugged her.

"I'm so glad you came," Lana said.

"Thanks for inviting me."

Shar hugged her too. "It's great you could join us. The more the merrier."

"I was more than ready to have some girl time," Kelsey admitted.

Shar and Lana agreed.

From the back of the building, Olivia and Jessica entered just as Cali and Jillian reached the bottom of the stairs. Everyone greeted each other with laughter and hugs. They were all excited to hang out together for the evening.

Kelsey felt blessed to be included.

She noticed that Shar wore a colorful T-shirt that said Save a Sea Turtle. She admired Shar for the work she did with the Windswept Bay Sea Turtle Hospital and the foundation that she'd started with her husband Gage. She planned to go visit it soon.

"I'm going to come out and ride at some point," Shar said. "I just haven't found the time yet. But I will be out soon to jog the beach in search of sea turtle nests, or clutches as they're called. Bess used to always let me know if she spotted any. She always would put up the protective tape to warn people to stay away. I can come out and show you how to do that, if you don't mind."

"I would love that. I have to be honest. I don't know much about sea turtles since I've never lived near the ocean before."

"Shar is the one to show you how to do all that," Jessica said. "She's like Superwoman. She saves the day for a sea turtle all the time. Everyone told me that but now I know it's true."

Shar laughed. "I do what I can to save a turtle."

"Yes, you do," Cali said. "More than most."

"That's true," Jillian said.

"I think that is wonderful," Kelsey said. "I think it would be wonderful for the stable to foster some wild Mustangs."

"Oh, we should do that," Lana said. "My brothers actually are involved in a program for saving wild Mustangs. I'll ask Cam about us doing some here.

They can use as much help as possible."

"That's a great idea," Shar said. "I'm all for saving the animals. Who runs that program?"

"It's the Bureau of Land Management," Kelsey said. "I've always hoped there was a way for me to help them. But I've never actually owned land enough to help."

"We're going to make it happen," Lana said. "That beach is crying out for some American wild heritage to lope along its shoreline."

Everyone smiled at that and began talking excitedly. Kelsey liked everyone that much more. She had missed so much hanging out with friends.

All of her life—before her dad died—she and her mom had moved from place to place, following him wherever the military sent him. She would make friends and then leave them behind. Because of this, she'd found it hard as an adult to ever really connect with many people for extended friendships. Her own career had moved her around a good bit. But now, here on Windswept Bay's shores, she was excited about staying and setting down roots. All the more reason she didn't want trouble to follow her here.

This was her new beginning. Not just with her job but with her life. It was a place she knew in her heart she could settle and stay forever. She felt safe, or at least had felt safe until her ex-boss had shown up. And Cam Sinclair was one of the most outstanding and well-respected men she knew and the perfect boss. He was madly, deeply in love with Lana so she didn't have to worry about any of the junk she'd had to worry about with her last job. This was the perfect setup for her.

If only her jerk of an ex-boss didn't do anything more to mess it up. Thankfully she hadn't seen him anymore and that was a good thing.

To her surprise, Max had called twice over the last few days, just to ask her whether everything was okay and to make sure her ex hadn't bothered her anymore. She had thought that was nice of him for doing so and she had to admit that each time he called and each time she saw his name on her phone and then heard the sound of his voice, a thrill of anticipation hit her. It was different from the anticipation she'd felt about coming here to spend the evening out with girlfriends…it was so very different. Oh, she tried to tell herself it wasn't happening but it was very clear that he had captured her interest. She was holding steady, staying strong, and had kept their conversations strictly about him checking on her safety and welfare. They had been friendly but he was respecting her wishes and there was no talk about dating or any of that.

That didn't stop her from thinking about it…nor had it stopped her from thinking about him. Nor had it stopped her from wondering all day long how his appointment at the doctor had gone today.

Pushing that out of her mind, she tried not to let it intrude on this moment. She couldn't let herself get emotionally involved with Max and that meant she couldn't have him on her mind constantly.

"So shall we go to the patio?" Cali asked everyone. "They are holding a corner table on the patio for us overlooking the water. It should be a lovely night to sit and enjoy it and have a good time."

"Our own little world for the evening." Olivia

smiled.

"Perfect," Shar said and everybody agreed. They followed Cali out the back doors of the lobby. The area was beautiful, even in the diminishing sunlight; with the lights coming on, the landscaping was gorgeous.

She couldn't help remarking on it. "This resort is beautiful. The flowers are so lovely."

Shar grinned and pointed at Jillian. "That's our Jillian. She has a green thumb—I have a black thumb. I think she stole my green part too, but I'm okay with that. Yep, she does all this. With the crew, but it all comes out of that pretty head of hers. I've always said we are very lucky to have her."

Jillian shook her head, looking embarrassed at her sister's beaming compliments. "I love what I do and you know, it's kind of like being an artist. I see it in my head and then reproduce it here. But it's not just me. I have such a talented crew. I think you might have met Blair. She is our number-one employee; she'll do anything she can to help out. But she's my right-hand woman and helps keep everything running smoothly. She's pregnant right now, too, and has to slow down a little bit. I don't know what I'm going to do when she goes part-time for the first six months and then I do the same two months later."

"We will make it," Cali said. "You and these two babies will be what's important!"

Immediately everyone started talking excitedly about the babies. They seemed as excited for their friend Blair and her husband Jax as they were for Jillian and her husband Ryan. Kelsey thought that was sweet and she loved how much they cared. There was a small hope that when she…if she…ever found love and was expecting a child that she would finally have true friends like these who would be thrilled for her. Kelsey just hadn't realized how much she craved all of these connections.

Or had realized exactly how isolated she'd become.

Jillian explained that Jax owned the Lagoon Adventures in town and also worked with Cali's husband as an artist. Cali's husband was the world-famous sea life painter Grant Ellington. He traveled the world, painting huge sea life murals, and from what she understood, Jax went with him sometimes for bigger projects. Kelsey knew that to paint with Grant was an honor and it meant that Jax must be talented himself.

Grant had given him a great opportunity. It made Kelsey think of the great opportunity that Cam was giving her. The opportunity to start over. Fresh.

"So, we're hoping Jillian's baby has a green thumb like Jillian so the tradition can be carried on," Olivia said.

"I don't have a green thumb." Kelsey laughed. "But if I did, I never really have the time or take the time to plant much and really haven't been in any place in a while where I could take the liberty of planting anything. I'm excited about being here working for Cam." She looked at Lana. "I am so grateful for your fiancé and the opportunity that he's given me. I'm loving getting to know all of you."

Lana gave her a quick hug. "Believe me, we are so grateful for you. Because of you, he can be in Texas and know that things will be great here."

It felt so good to be appreciated. It gave her a

content feeling to know that she was appreciated and it was something that she had lacked for a long time.

They ordered appetizers and drinks as the live singer in the corner of the deck played his guitar and sang old Beach Boy tunes and an array of other hit songs from the past. The atmosphere was perfect and the company excellent. As the sisters and sisters-in-law and soon-to-be sisters-in-law chattered happily, Kelsey couldn't help but think that if she was ever going to be in a family unit, this would be a great family to marry into. The thought struck her out of the blue, startling her and sending her thoughts instantly back to Max.

His handsome face filled her mind, and that dimple appeared as he smiled. Her chest fluttered and she groaned silently. The man invaded her thoughts and sent her heart pounding simply thinking about him. It was not a good thing for a gal determined not to get involved with a military man.

What a cruel twist of fate.

Still, as she sat there, she looked around and realized that none of his sisters knew the struggle that Max was going through right now. None of them knew that the career he loved and was so dedicated to, the life he had chosen and loved, could very well have ended for him today. With that thought in her mind, there was no way she could get him off her mind for the rest of the evening…no matter how much she knew she couldn't get involved with him.

Two days later, she hadn't heard from him and she couldn't help but worry that he was sitting home, hurting, and that he'd gotten bad news.

Because of the guilt she felt over the whole incident, worrying about him was almost too much to take. She didn't sleep much that night and when she woke, there was just no getting away from it…she had to go check on him.

She took two separate groups riding on the beach. She loved riding her horse on the beach and listening to the excited chatter of the people in the group but her heart wasn't in it. It was a beautiful sunny day: the white, pristine, sandy beach with water so beautiful and blue, glistening like jewels in the sparkling sunlight. The backdrop of swaying palm trees and beautiful native underbrush and a blue cloudless sky hanging above them…it was truly paradise. But today all she could think about was Max.

She kept looking at her phone, thinking that he would call. It had been so long and maybe he would call and check up on her. But he didn't.

When the last tour was over, it was just after lunch and she could not stand it any longer. "Zack," she called to one of the college students who worked for her. "I'm going to take the afternoon off. Can you handle it?"

"Sure. No problem."

"Thanks." She kept it short, not wanting him to ask any questions, and headed inside to grab a quick shower. She might be worried about Max but she wasn't going to show up at his house smelling of horse. Thirty minutes later, she climbed into her truck and decided to call him before she reached his place. It would be better to do that than surprise him. But her call went unanswered and that solidified her decision to drive out there. Her gut told her something wasn't right.

She drove to town and on down the beach road that led to his place. When she reached his gate, it was, of course, locked. So she parked her truck, took the keys and then hopped over the fence. She walked down the lane and around the corner—and gasped. She hadn't seen his place in the daylight. It was beautiful: a private cove with a small beach that had a small, faded red wooden boat turned upside down in the sand out of reach of the tide…but waiting to be turned over and taken for a ride.

A handful of colorful deck chairs sat near it, also out of reach of the incoming tide. Max's place might be small but it had loads of character. She smiled when she saw the cute, blue shack nestled into the trees. She expected Charlotte to run up as she approached and was surprised when the pig didn't come out. It didn't come around when she knocked on the door either. There was no pig and no Max. *But his truck was there...* She looked around, half expecting him to suddenly walk out of the tropical woods.

Then she heard hammering. She turned in that

direction, toward the trees. The land just past the bungalow went upward at a fairly steep angle, something she hadn't seen in the darkness, even with the bright moon since the trees shadowed it. Her breath caught suddenly. There was a house up there.

Or at least the beginnings of a house.

Max was building a house.

He'd told her he was improving the place and that he was doing all the work, which meant it took awhile—she hadn't realized he hadn't been talking about this little blue shack. He'd been talking about this. *What a project.*

She followed the path that led up to the house. It was beautiful, not finished but the exterior had come together and blended in with the trees. It was made of stone, wood, and glass. He would have an amazing view from this level, overlooking the water.

There was no door yet and so she entered through the unframed doorway and looked toward the sound of hammering. She saw him across the room with his back to her. He was working on framing in a wall. He wore a tool belt, slung low on his jean-clad hips, and a dark-navy T-shirt. Charlotte sat at his feet, practically lounging on his boots as she watched his every move with interest.

So did Kelsey. She took a step toward him and both he and Charlotte turned toward her, the man and his pig. Charlotte squealed, jump to her hooves and trotted toward Kelsey. Her little piggy tail did some serious shaking.

Obviously Charlotte was happy to see her but Max wasn't smiling.

No, his expression told her exactly what she had been afraid to know.

"I was worried about you." She studied him as she rubbed Charlotte's ears. "I thought I'd come check on you."

His jaw stiffened and his eyes shifted away.

"So…how are you?" she asked, more determined than ever to make the stubborn man talk.

He looked back at her. "It wasn't good," he said, with almost no emotion in his voice.

That lack of emotion also told her how hard the news had been for him. "So you're out? It's over?"

He gave a curt nod. "Yeah, and it's the only decision they can make. Of course, they offered me a desk job, but I turned it down. I am taking the discharge. They say it's the only thing that they could do…it really was the only option. I can't be responsible for potentially hurting one of my team members. They put their lives in my hands, and I put my life in their hands. I would expect the same of them. It's that cut-and-dried. Just like you pointed out."

She hurt for him. It didn't matter that her view was that she couldn't handle the life of a military family. No, this was about Max. And the fact that Max was hurting. She was shocked at how much it hurt her for him. *Was this how her dad had felt? Or would have felt if he'd gotten out? Maybe.* That didn't change how she'd felt as his child.

"I'm really sorry. So what will you do?"

He gave a gruff, dry laugh. "I'll build this house. I've been working on my little project for a long time. I'll have surgery on my knee. I think it's going to happen next week."

"I knew that your family didn't know what you were going through. And I had dinner with your sisters and also Lana and Jessica night before last. It just weighed on me that no one knew what was happening with you and I came out to check on you. To see how you were doing. I hope you don't mind."

"No, I don't mind. I'm not in a very good mood. But then I'm also not going to let myself wallow in my disappointment. I'm alive. I can't say that about everybody. Not everyone comes back from these missions."

It was the closest he'd come to letting her in on anything about his missions. And it struck her then that in this mission where his knee had been hurt so badly, that had ended his career…others must not have come home.

And that hurt him.

"I've been thinking about that a lot. About you and your dad. I really do get the decision and your reasoning. But now, I can't say much, but I went to some funerals when I got back from the last mission. And it was rough watching my buddies' families…their children. And you went through that. You understand more than most."

She wanted to wrap her arms around him and give him comfort that she knew he wasn't asking for. Or was she sure he would welcome it. But she wanted to anyway. And then again, that was dangerous for her. "I came because I do understand, despite everything. I understand."

They stared at each other for a long time. She took a deep breath. The urge to wrap her arms around him was almost overwhelming. So much so that she took a step back so that she wouldn't follow through. "I guess I just want to say…I'm here. I'm here if you want to talk. I know there's things you can't talk about, but I'm here. And also, you're going to tell your family now? Right?"

"Yeah, I'm going to tell them. I just needed time to process. I'll tell them tomorrow probably."

She nodded. She wasn't the only one to give him consolation then. He would have others who understood. Others who could support him. And he would have his brothers. Other men who he could lean on.

"I guess I better go. I need to get back to the stable. I just couldn't help but come by." Unable to stop herself, she crossed to him and stopped a few feet from him. He looked startled as she took the final step and wrapped her arms around him. Her heart thundered in her chest. She could not help laying her head on his chest. She felt his heart beating rapidly against her ear as his arms came around her. He said nothing and she said nothing; then she let go of him and backed out of his arms. "I'll see you later."

She started to walk away.

"How did you get here?"

She turned. "I walked. I parked my truck at the entrance."

"Oh, okay. And here I thought I was blocking out the world."

She laughed. "It's just in your mind. You have plenty of folks out there who wouldn't let you block them out for too long."

"Yeah, that's true. Thanks for coming."

She noticed he wasn't moving. And she wondered

how bad his knee was hurting. But right now she had a feeling that his knee wasn't what was hurting him the worst. The fact that his career had ended before he was ready for it to end was probably a much higher intensity of pain than his leg.

"Take care of yourself." She walked out the door and down the path, her thoughts heavy as she saw the blue water and then walked to her truck.

The thought hit her then. *In his pain, in his loss, it had also opened the door and taken away all the barriers that she had put in place between them.*

CHAPTER SEVEN

After Kelsey left, Max set his hammer down, and then hopped over to the open window and eased himself down onto the windowsill. He grunted with the pain. He had almost decided not to have the surgery but there was a lot messed up in there and the doctors had advised that he go through with it now and not wait. His knee was so shredded the doctors were worried that he would never have a hundred percent recovery. Even after surgery, he could have stability issues. These doctors wondered why the prior doctors who'd looked at his knee right after the mission had not done surgery immediately.

He hadn't lost a limb or his life, so he should be grateful. And he was. He just had to get over his shock and accept that life as he'd known it was over and it was time to plan a new future.

He stood and reached for the cane that he had been using and then walked slowly out the side entrance of the house and sank to the seat of his all-terrain vehicle. The only way he'd managed to get up the hill was using his ATV. Now he felt guilty that he hadn't offered to take Kelsey back to her truck but he hadn't wanted her to feel any worse than she probably already did. She was already worried that she'd made his injury worse. If she had seen him hobbling around, she would be horrified. He would not put that on her.

He drove down the hill and Charlotte trotted beside the vehicle. He parked right outside his bungalow and he moved straight from the ATV to his truck. There was no sense wasting any more time. It was time to go see his family. Time to admit that he had a problem.

Time to let them know that he would not have

their pity. It was already over and done and time to move on.

He stopped by the police station first, spotting Levi's SUV and Jillian's husband Ryan's too. He'd been an undercover cop for years and had had to give it up, so in some respects he'd been through what Max was going through. Only, Ryan had been ready for a change.

Max knew Ryan was very happy and they were expecting a baby soon.

He needed to adjust like that; he knew he was going to have to try to adjust like Ryan. He got out of his seat and grabbed his cane. He needed to get a crutch and after he told his family, he would probably go pick one up. There was no need to try to hide it now and he didn't know whether he could make it a week till surgery without one.

"Hey, brother." Levi looked surprised when he saw the cane. "*What* is that?"

Ryan put down his pen. "Did you hurt yourself?"

"Well, not exactly. I've been hurt since I got back from my last mission. I was able to hide it until I jumped out of the truck to help Kelsey last week. I need to have surgery next week."

"How bad is it? How long will recovery take?" Levi asked.

"It's gonna take awhile, and at best, it will only be a seventy percent recovery due to the complexities of the injury. The doctors gave me the news yesterday."

Ryan and Levi looked at each other and he saw their minds working. "Yeah, I got my walking papers yesterday."

"That's too bad." Ryan shook his head.

Levi's brows dipped. "You're out? They're letting you go?" His words were a mixture of disbelief and concern.

"Yeah. No choice. You know I need to be a hundred percent."

"Understandable," Ryan muttered, thinking. "Still, I know that's rough for you."

"Yeah. It's rough."

"If it's any consolation," Ryan offered, "for me, there was life after undercover. As for you, there will be life after Special Ops if you let there be."

"So I hear." His thoughts went to Kelsey. "I've been in denial since I got back but I've been pretty sure this was coming. Even before my stunt the other night when Kelsey's boss showed up."

"Here, have a seat." Levi went around the desk and turned the chair so Max wouldn't have to walk too far.

Max eased down into the chair, the brace helping to keep his knee straight. Still, he grimaced.

"Maybe you should have sat on the desk so it wouldn't have been so low." Levi looked concerned.

"It's fine. And I'm fine…really. I'm coming to terms with it. Kelsey made a point the other night that if I wasn't a hundred percent physically that I endangered my team. That really helped me see a new perspective."

Both Ryan's and Levi's eyes filled with speculation as he realized what he'd said.

"So you and Kelsey are talking?" Levi asked.

"Yeah, we are," he said with hesitancy, trying to decide how much to reveal. "I like her. She has a good head on her shoulders. Cam did good when he hired her. What a joke for a boss—ex-boss she had. What I'd like to do to him…" Hostility toward the man was something that was going to be hard to get over. He wanted to protect her. "Speaking of, she tells me that he hasn't been back around. Do you think this is over? Or do you think he's going to show back up?"

"Well, let's just say I have a patrol car making a patrol out there a few times a day. I've told Cam about it. Ryan and I did some research on him. And he is not the kind of guy who gives up real easy on something he wants. And he is not all that well thought of in the circles he travels in. So I don't know. He's putting himself in jeopardy by getting his name drug through a lawsuit. But he's hot enough that that might not matter. So if she's not pressing charges, we're in a wait-and-see holding pattern."

"You stay out of trouble," Ryan added.

"Well, at the moment, I'm fairly useless. I had a little movement left in me the other day but that's pretty much gone by the wayside for now. So, I'm going to have to rely on you guys to make sure she's safe."

"We are doing all we can. I hate it that she didn't press charges on him."

"Yeah, me too, and I told her so. I can still protect her with my weapons if I needed to but…"

"I'd appreciate if you would try to refrain from being involved. I'll try to keep her safe."

"Try isn't good enough." Max held his brother's gaze. "Keep her safe."

"We are doing everything we can. She did not sign a restraining order, so I can't arrest the man for walking up to her or to the stables. Or approaching her in town. She didn't give me the grounds to do that. Still, I will make sure she's safe. You care about this girl," Levi said. "I don't think I've ever seen you this serious before."

"Yeah, you're right. I have to say there is something about her that had me at hello. That's a movie cliché, I know, but it's true."

Ryan grinned. "That's how it works sometimes."

He nodded. "But her dad was a Marine. He died for our country and she's not into military men."

Levi's expression turned speculative. "You're not

in the military anymore."

"Yeah, so I've been told."

Kelsey was upset more than she wanted to be when she left Max's place. She wasn't ready to go back to the stables but wasn't sure where to go. Then she spotted the Windswept Bay Sea Turtle Hospital. Without another thought, she pulled into the parking lot and got out.

It was the perfect distraction.

She was just walking toward the entrance when she saw through the open gate a group of people exit the building and head toward one of the ambulances. Shar was one of them. Without stopping to think, Kelsey stepped through the open gate and walked toward them.

Shar spotted her. "Hey, Kelsey, you came by."

"Yeah, I thought I'd check it out. Are you going somewhere?"

"We've got a turtle in trouble. You want to come?"

She needed a distraction and this was certainly that. "Sure. If I won't be in the way."

A good-looking guy with curly dark hair was opening the back of the ambulance. "Are you kidding? That's Shar's code way of saying come help us."

Shar laughed. "Alex is right. We can always use help."

Alex pulled out a bag and strapped it on his back. Shar pulled a tub from the back of the ambulance.

Excitement filled Kelsey. "Then I'd love to come along."

The other man—John, Shar called him—closed the doors to the ambulance. "Follow them," he said.

Kelsey realized that Shar and Alex were headed toward the back of the building. Toward the water.

To her surprise, within moments, she was in a power boat with the Sea Turtle Hospital emblem on the side. Alex stood at the wheel; John stood beside him. She and Shar sat on a bench at the back of the boat as they sped across the sparkling blue water. Sea spray rose and splashed her, feeling refreshing and shocking as the wind whipped around them. Anticipation filled her at the very thought of participating in a rescue.

"It's a loggerhead sea turtle and it's bleeding and floundering in the water about five miles out between the shore and the reef. Jake spotted it and called in the coordinates. He was taking a group out to dive at the reef. It very well could have been hit by a boat propeller or bitten by a shark."

"Is it big?"

Shar shrugged. "Jake said it looked to be over two hundred pounds at least. Loggerheads grow to around four hundred pounds, so not as large as some species. Big enough that it may take all of us to get it in or the crane."

They slowed when they reached an area and spotted a diver's flag that Jake had set out. Sure enough, not far away was the bobbing injured turtle. It was still alive.

"Why didn't Jake try to save it?"

"We prefer to be notified. Especially if they are big like this."

Alex maneuvered the boat and John leaned out as they approached. "It's three hundred for sure. It's a big boy."

Alex lined the boat's backend toward the turtle and John and Shar stepped out onto the deck. John pulled off his shirt, exposing his muscled chest—the rescue worker obviously kept in shape.

He grinned as he tossed his shirt. "Someone always has to go in," he teased.

"And he loves it," Shar said. "He gets to flex his muscles and rescue a sea turtle. Only, no flexing at Kelsey, John. Max might hurt you."

John looked surprised. "Really, you and Max?"

Kelsey looked from Shar's mischievously twinkling eyes to John's speculative gaze. "He's a good friend." She refused to elaborate.

Shar grinned. "Okay, let's do this," she said, suddenly all serious and putting the focus back on the rescue.

Alex brought the large tub with low sides and hooked it to the metal mechanized L-shaped wench on the back of the boat. He swung it out and lowered it to the water. John slipped into the water and Shar moved closer to the edge. She motioned to Kelsey to step out onto the deck.

Kelsey did as she was asked and they watched as John eased in behind the huge turtle and pushed it gently toward the bucket that Alex and Shar held steady from two different angles.

"You just be ready to grab where possible to help pull it into the bucket," Shar told her.

As soon as the turtle met the open lip of the bucket, she saw Alex's muscled arms tense as he held the back end steady and Shar helped pull the turtle inside. Kelsey reached out and grabbed the slick edge of the shell and pulled. All of them together were able to get the huge turtle into the container. Then Alex pushed the button and they helped guide the container into the low-sided boat and set it down in the floor. John was back on deck in a split second and they all were inside. Alex and John went to work on the wound.

"Shark bite," Shar observed.

"It's an old one. I'm thinking he's been in trouble and floating in with the tide for a couple of days," Alex said. "Let's get him to the hospital."

Kelsey sat back down, out of the way. It was clear they didn't need her now. Within seconds, they were speeding back across the water.

Kelsey was fascinated by the entire process. After they reached the shore, they had the turtle unloaded and into the back of an ATV. Once at the hospital, they moved it to a stretcher and into surgery.

Shar hugged her. "You did great. Don't you feel awesome knowing you helped rescue the turtle?"

Kelsey did. She'd been a part of saving an almost endangered sea turtle. "I do. I totally get why you love this."

Shar looked satisfied. "I love it. I'm obsessed by it. Thankfully, Gage gets it and has been such a help to the project by helping me form our foundation. It enables me to help all the more with awareness."

"Let me know how it goes. I'll come back out to see him."

"What are you going to name him? The rescuer gets to name it."

"Oh, me?"

Shar nodded. "Yes, you."

Thoughts rolled through Kelsey's mind. She thought of Max and wished he'd been here to see it. She wondered whether he'd been involved in any rescues. Pushing thoughts of him away, she focused. "How about Wilbur? In *Charlotte's Web*, Wilbur the pig survived because of the help of his friends."

Shar chuckled. "Thinking of Max?"

Kelsey's cheeks heated. "Maybe."

"Hey, I love it. My brother needs someone. Speaking of Charlotte and Wilbur, I pointed out to him that he got the pig's name wrong when he named the pig Charlotte and not Wilbur. He pointed out his pig is a female so he didn't feel right naming her Wilbur."

Kelsey smiled. "Charlotte fits his pig. She worries over him like Charlotte worried over Wilbur in the book, so it works."

"Yes, that pig loves my brother and that's part of the problem…Max needs a woman to love him."

Kelsey had that on her mind as she drove away from the hospital. *Max did need someone to love him…*

Her heart squeezed tight at the thought. She was in new, uncharted territory.

CHAPTER EIGHT

After leaving Levi and Ryan's office, he drove to find Trent. Trent had been in the military also and had not reenlisted. Trent did not talk about his military life. Trent built things. *What was about them and doing things with their hands?* Trent built homes and he enjoyed remodeling, taking something that was old and making it new. He also had started building extravagant tree houses lately. Max thought that Trent would be a great candidate for a DIY show like they had on television. Problem was Trent was not the most talkative; he was the quietest of all of them even quieter than Max. And some of that quietness had come after he'd gotten out of the military. Their sisters had renovated the resort and had asked Trent to be in charge of it. But Trent had turned them down, had told them that if they could get the work done at a reasonable price he would rather they did that. Trent didn't like taking on huge jobs and the renovation of the resort had been a big job. It was still going on. Everyone had respected Trent's decision to turn the job down…no one pushed.

He lived more inland, not on the beach but he had a view from his hilltop and was happy where he was. Said he could go to the beach whenever he wanted but liked living in the area he lived in. He liked living in the trees.

The cool thing about where Trent lived was that it was downstream from the waterfall. So instead of the sound of the surf, he had the peaceful, quiet sound of a bubbling stream in his backyard.

Max found him there, working on his motorcycle. "Hey," he said as he walked up.

"You hurt yourself worse?"

"Worse?" Max studied him. "You knew?"

Trent tightened a bolt on the engine and shot him a squint. "Yeah, I knew. But I figured if you had wanted to say something, you would. I knew you were hurting and I saw the swelling around your knee—your jeans were tight there. I figured whenever you were ready you would say something. But you never did. It was your business."

"Yeah, my business. I was discharged yesterday."

Trent stopped working. "Sorry, man. I know that's hard on you."

He shrugged. "Yeah, I'm dealing. I'm making my rounds, telling everyone."

"Mom will be sad for you, but overjoyed. She won't be able to hide it. Neither will the sisters."

"I figured that."

"They can stop worrying now. Never knowing. It's hard for women. But they didn't hold you back because they love you."

"You sound like you have experience with that."

"A little, but it's also understandable. While I was in, I got to be the one who worried. Got to experience it from the other perspective. My girlfriend was going out on a different mission than I was. I...got to experience the worry, the fear."

Max didn't know what to say about that. Trent had never talked this much about his time in the service.

"I also experienced what it was like to lose somebody."

Max stared at him. "Aw, man, I'm sorry." So now he knew why his brother didn't talk about it. He hadn't wanted to talk about it.

"Yeah, so give your mom and the girls a break if they show their true emotions. They try to hide it but you feel it."

"Are you okay?"

Trent nodded. "I've learned to live with it."

"I'm sorry you've had to go through this alone."

"Jake has always known. When I first got back, I was in a bad way and he found me one night. I had had a little more to drink than I should have and spilled my guts to him. So he's known but kept it to himself."

"Well, I'm glad you had somebody. It helps to

have someone to talk to."

He'd learned that. Kelsey had helped him. "So I'm going to be adjusting. I've got to figure out what I'm going to do."

Trent grinned at him. "Well, you know Jake is always looking for a dive master. Divers seemed to move around faster than surfers. If you want to do that."

"I might take a few to help him out. I won't be taking it on full-time. I don't love it like Jake. I might also go into business. I was thinking about a security business. I've been throwing a lot of things around. I could also build furniture."

"Give yourself time—you'll figure it out."

"You ever going to get that thing rebuilt?"

He laughed. "A man's got to have a hobby, you know. She's almost rebuilt. She's a beauty, isn't she?"

"Vintage." It was a 1937 Knucklehead, one of the record-setting machines back in the day when it was created and very coveted. Trent had bought it from a lady a couple of years ago who'd found it in her barn.

He'd been working on it ever since.

"So I would ask if you want to go surfing but that would be cruel."

Max shook his head. "Hit me where it hurts, man. Have some pity on me."

Trent laughed. "Man, you're a Marine. Once a Marine, always a Marine. We don't give up. We don't stop. We move on. We take what we've got and we deal with it. You'll do that. And you'll be happy. It's not good when a man doesn't accept it. It's not good at all. I see strain in your eyes and I have a feeling that you're in a lot of pain right now. Get the surgery and be done with it. Move on, be happy. Start a family. You thought about that?"

"Hey, where's your family?"

Trent shrugged. "I'm not opposed to it but it takes two. I haven't found that one yet. From what I see, you haven't even been looking."

"Yeah, honestly, I've been thinking about it. Was starting to think about it before this mission. I'll adjust—it just might take time. Might have to open up a little." Max thought about that. He had worked with his thoughts and what he talked about on lock down for so long that he'd tended to lock down everything and Trent knew it. He'd locked his gates, his heart… Maybe it was time he did some unlocking.

Trent gave him an understanding look. "You'll be okay, man. So when is surgery?"

"Next week. Then recovery. I'm ready to be able to move around but first I'll have to get through that."

"Well, you know Mom and the sisters will probably kill you with casseroles and checking on you."

If there was one thing Max knew, it was that there would not be a shortage of family trying to take care of him. "Yeah, you might have to come share a meal or two with me."

"If they bring lasagna, I'm coming to take it."

"Ha! If they bring lasagna, I'll share it but you're not taking it. I won't be that down and out." They both chuckled over that.

He hoped it would be as easy as Trent made adjusting and moving on sound. Time would tell. And a few minutes later, as he left, his thoughts went to Kelsey.

Kelsey was startled a couple days later when Max showed up.

She was coming out of a barn when he drove into the yard. Her heart did its thing and she told it to stop but she remembered that Max was not in the military anymore. Her excuse for not getting involved with him was not there any longer.

She strode toward him, her boots crunching on the gravel but she almost didn't hear it for the beating of her heart.

"Hey there." She watched him ease out of the truck. He reached inside and pulled out a cane. Then, with his back leaning against the truck, he used the cane to take all the pressure off his knee. She could only imagine how much his knee was hurting. The man was more stubborn than a mule. "Don't you have surgery tomorrow?"

"Yeah, I leave early. I'll be there overnight. Then

I'll be moving slow again for a little while."

"But then you'll start getting well. I know you're all macho and you've trained to be tough, but Max, I can tell you're in pain. Why are you driving? Why are you here when it's obvious you're hurting?"

"You are the most observant person. It's not that apparent."

"Ha, wrong. Do not deny it."

He shot her a rueful look. "Okay, yes, it's getting worse. I even had to take some painkillers at night. But I don't have to let it rule me. I came to ask you if you might consider going to dinner tonight."

"Dinner? You're kidding, right?"

"No. I want to take you to dinner."

"You're in pain—"

"We have already established that fact. So let's move forward…will you go to dinner with me?"

She almost chuckled he was so put out by her worry over him. "I really don't think that is a good idea."

"You are the most stubborn woman—"

"Me? You're the one hurting."

"And I'd like something to take my mind off that fact. Dinner with you is exactly what I need."

She sighed. She should turn him down—she should. But why?

Because what I'm feeling for him scares me.

The voice in her head was right. She had fought it and fought it, but she knew that the connection that she had with Max was stronger than anything she had ever felt for anyone. And now that the barrier that had been between them was lifted, there was no reason for her not to face up to that fear. *Was there?*

She could go out with him and enjoy herself if he could go out with her while suffering.

He squinted at her. "You had to think about it that hard? I'm not in the military anymore."

She swallowed the lump of trepidation lodged in her windpipe and then blew out a slow, steady breath. "I…had to think about it because you and I both know that something is going on between us."

His lip hitched slowly to one side. "I've known that for a while. I've been thinking about it ever since we talked the other day. The only thing that I see positive about my military career ending is that there is nothing left standing in the way of us."

Her stomach dipped. *Oh dear goodness, she was in trouble.* "I've been thinking about that."

"It's all I've been thinking about."

Her heart squeezed. "Sooo, I guess if I didn't have to clean house tonight, I could say yes."

His brows crinkled. "Huh? You are not going to choose house cleaning—"

She laughed. "I'm teasing. I'll go as long as it's somewhere you won't have to work too hard to get to. And then don't have to move around a lot."

"You mean like a drive-in?"

"Sure, perfect."

He frowned. "While I like a good hamburger myself, that's not exactly what I was thinking. Though dressing up would be a stretch…that's why I'm wearing shorts today."

"Maybe we should forget it and you just come in and put some ice on it."

"While nothing sounds more thrilling than you putting an ice pack on my knee, I think I'll pass. I'd like to at least take you to a restaurant. We could go back to Paradise Grill. It's a small parking lot and easy access."

She was touched by how much he wanted to take her out. He had to be hurting. "That sounds like the perfect plan. And it has a great atmosphere." And it was the place she'd first laid eyes on him.

He looked at his watch. "Can you go now?"

"Now?"

He nodded. "Am I being too pushy?"

Her lips twitched. "Extremely. But it's okay. I can go if you give me a few minutes to wash the horse smell off of me. You'll thank me and so will the others at the restaurant."

"Sounds good to me. I'll chill on the couch."

It didn't take her long, though she hurried as fast as she could, knowing that speed would help her not back out of going. That may have been his whole reasoning for hurrying her into the date.

Which was actually a nice feeling. He really wanted to spend time with her.

They arrived at the Paradise Grill and Bert led them out onto the back deck to a table near the entrance, which made Max not have to walk any farther than necessary.

Kelsey had tried to get him to stay inside because it was a shorter walk but he'd insisted it was too beautiful a night to stay inside. He didn't care if his leg fell off; he was having a romantic dinner under the stars with this woman. She was making it almost impossible. She insisted they be as close to the door as possible if she agreed to a longer walk and he finally gave in. Bert, the owner and a friend, didn't even try to hide his grin as he watched them argue quietly with each other. And he chuckled when Max finally gave in.

"The table near the door then." Max laughed at last. "Whatever it takes to get the woman on the deck works for me."

"I was wondering when you were going to wise

up, dude. She's tougher than any football lineup you and me used to face down on the team."

He chuckled. He and Bert, along with most of his brothers, had played high school football together. Bert had gone on to play college ball and though Max had been given an offer, he'd turned it down and gone into the Marines.

"You're right about that."

Kelsey hitched a brow and smiled. "I'm just holding you to our agreement we made before I agreed to the date."

"It's true," he told Bert, who laughed.

"You two have a lovely evening. Try not to argue as you chill. The waitress will be here soon. If he gives you any trouble, call me." He winked at Kelsey.

Max grinned and rubbed his knee. "He's a good guy."

"I like him, and I like his place. It's perfect."

"I think my date is perfect."

She met his eyes with almost disbelieving eyes.

"Why do you look like that?"

"I wasn't expecting it."

"A compliment? I don't know why not. I find everything about you special. And I'm not kidding."

She let her long fingers play with the edge of the menu that Bert had placed in front of each of them before he left.

"Does that bother you?"

"No, well." Her eyes wavered from his and then came back. "A little. I'm honestly having to adjust to the idea of you not being military. I had all this resistance and boundary walls up and now I can take them down."

"I hope so," he said.

The singer in the far corner of the deck started to sing the Kenny Chesney song "When the Sun Goes Down." They were both quiet for a moment, listening.

"He's good," she said after a few moments.

Kelsey finally looked as though she was relaxing. A feeling of contentment eased over him like the warm glow of sunshine on a cold day as he studied her.

"You are beautiful, you know."

She had been looking out at the dark ocean. "Thank you."

"I figured if I say it again you'll get used to hearing it and be more comfortable."

She smiled as if she thought he was slightly crazy. "I think I like hearing that from you."

"Well, now we're talking. Because I like saying it. And I refuse to let some jerk mess up my right to compliment my date."

"Oh, now that's true. He was a jerk."

"Do you have a lot of men in your profession acting like jerks to you?"

She shook her head. "There are always jerks in any profession, but you can usually get around that. Unless you work for them and live on their property. What a mistake. I should have run the moment I realized what a jerk he was. Big mistake on my part. Live and learn."

"Yeah, sadly—though you shouldn't have to learn."

"But I can't let it taint my view of everyone. Look at Cam. I'm living on his property and I have no worry that he's going to make a pass at me. Some men are still gentlemen and faithful."

"Yeah, Cam is so in love with Lana there is no chance of that happening. I'm going to tell you straight up that I'm not going to be a jerk. I'm going to do my best to treat you like the lady you are."

The waitress came and took their orders and after she left, Kelsey leaned forward. "Okay, back to the conversation. Well, while I appreciate the sentiment about you treating me like a lady, I'm going to insist that you don't try to beat me to the truck door when we leave like you did earlier. I am quite capable of opening my own door and you are in no shape to do it right now."

"Hey, my knee is going to hurt me no matter what."

"You are a hardheaded man."

"Yes, I am. And I'm warning you, I'm not likely to change."

She held his gaze. "That goes for me too."

They studied each other as slow smiles spread across both their faces.

"I have a feeling our relationship won't be boring," he said, and was rewarded with another of her bubbling laughs. He could get addicted to her laugh—the sound made him feel as if everything in the world was right...or could be right. It just made him happy.

CHAPTER NINE

They talked all through dinner, aside from the times that the music was so good they just had to stop and listen. Those times, she caught him looking at her and he would give her a smile and then look back to the band. But those moments sent her heart flying.

By the time the meal was over, though, she sensed his knee was hurting worse. She'd learned to tell by the look in his eyes; they dulled and the crease between his eyebrows deepened.

"Do you want some of Bert's famous Hula Pie? Or some Key lime pie?"

"No. Thank you for the offer, but I believe it's time to get you home so you can put that knee up."

"I'm fine, if you want pie."

"I don't but get some if you want it."

"I have a sweet tooth but the truth is I was using pie as an excuse to extend my time with you."

"But you're hurting."

"So, what's new?"

"Okay." She raised her hand in surrender. "I have pie and coffee at home. And an ice pack. We will go back to my place and I'll feed you pie *while* we ice that knee down."

"I never thought I'd say this before I was an eighty-year-old man, but that is a really enticing idea. I like it. I like it a lot."

She laughed. "Then let's get out of here."

A few minutes later, they pulled up into Kelsey's yard. She looked at him skeptically. "Are you sure you want to get out?"

He opened his door. "Hey, I was promised pie and

an ice pack and I'm not eating after midnight, so that is a definite affirmative. I'm getting out and holding you to your offer."

"Then, by all means, let's get you iced down," she said, her pretty eyes clearly telling him she wasn't sure how to take him.

When they made it inside, he immediately headed toward the couch. "Sadly, the ice pack has me drooling more than the thought of pie."

"Well, hang on, surfer boy—one ice pack coming up." She headed into her kitchen and he was distracted from his pain by the sway of her hips in rhythm with the bounce of her pretty hair.

He had, he decided, the best seat in all the world. "Why did you call me surfer boy?"

She laughed as she opened the refrigerator, pausing to look his way. Even from the distance, he saw her eyes twinkle.

"You have two surfboards at your house. You aren't a surfer?"

He got it. "I am, or at least I used to be. My injury might end that too, but it won't kill me if I don't get to get back on a board. Now, if I don't get that pie and coffee you're working on, I might have a problem."

"Then you're okay because it won't take but a few minutes once I hand you this." She brought him the ice packs and leaned over to gently place one under his knee and one on top of it. It was all he could do not to run his fingers through the thick mane of hair that fell in a curtain between her and him. When she was finished, she pushed the hair out of the way and smiled.

"Is that better?" she asked, so close all he could think about was kissing her.

"Better," he muttered, wanting so much to kiss this woman who'd captured all of his attention.

"Then I'll be right back."

He watched her walk away again, clueless to what she did to him. He leaned his head back on the couch and let the relief of the cold ice work magic on dulling his pain as he listened to her move around in the kitchen. It was comforting…which was an odd thought for him—and yet he realized, it fit as much with how he felt about Kelsey as did the fact that she drove him nuts with wanting more from their relationship. A lot more.

"Here you go," she said moments later.

He opened his eyes, startled that she was back so soon. She held a tray with two plates of apple pie. The scent told him it was warmed and his mouth watered instantly at the sweet scent.

"Did you make this?" He took the plate from her.

She rolled her pretty eyes. "Though I'm tempted to tell you yes, I cannot tell a lie—I bought it. There was an adorable little girl helping at a bake sale outside the grocery store yesterday and I could not turn her down."

"That was nice of you and it makes this all the sweeter." He dipped his fork into the golden crust and took a bite. It was delicious. "Someone knows how to bake a pie."

She paused as she set her plate on the coffee table. "I thought you'd like it. I'll be right back with the coffee. How do you drink yours?"

"Black."

She picked up the mug and handed it to him. Then

she sat down in the chair across from the couch. He wanted her on the couch next to him but his iced-down knee left no room.

"I'll be ready for the surgery to be done and this knee on the mend. Next time I come to sit on your couch, I'm hoping you'll sit beside me instead of all the way over there."

She smiled. "That can be arranged."

His life had taken a drastic change but in that moment, looking at her pretty smile and the promise in her eyes, Max felt more content than he had in weeks.

CHAPTER TEN

When Max got ready to leave, Kelsey walked him out to the truck. She had had a wonderful night. They hadn't held hands. They hadn't kissed…but she wanted to kiss him. They hadn't even sat on the couch together, but she felt so close to Max. When they reached his truck, he placed his cane inside the truck and then he turned to her.

His expression was so serious, and she believed he was feeling all the things that she was feeling. Anticipation raced through her; her heartbeat increased, her pulse climbed and when he gently slid one arm around her waist and then tugged ever so slightly, giving her a good option to move toward him or to move away, she willingly stepped toward him. His hands slid around her and pulled her close to him. He let his back rest against the truck, helping relieve pressure on his knees, and then he cupped her face with one hand as his gaze searched hers.

She knew he was giving her the opportunity to move out of his embrace and to step away from him if she wanted to. But she was, in that moment, right where she wanted to be.

Anticipation filled her for his kiss and there was absolutely no way she was stepping away from him. She had no plans to resist him. As she looked into his eyes, he leaned forward and kissed her.

The hand cupping her face pushed into her hair as he deepened the kiss.

It was a moment that would stand in time forevermore. It was as if her heart met his heart. And she understood that if he had kissed her before she had known he was out of the military, this kiss would have changed everything. This kiss, the emotions that it pulled from her, would have given her the conflict of her life because she'd never felt this depth of emotion before. Military or no military, she would not have been able to step away. Her knees went weak and of their own accord, her arms went around his shoulders as he deepened the kiss.

Was this how her mother had felt about her dad? Was this how all those other military wives felt about their husbands? This was an emotion that was as unstoppable as his love and desire to serve his country.

Suddenly she felt dampness on her cheeks.

She swallowed hard and lifted her head. His fingers immediately came to her cheeks and his thumb wiped away her tears.

"Kelsey? What—what are you crying for?"

"I didn't know." Her voice trembled. "I didn't understand."

His brows met and his gaze searched deeper. "Didn't know what, darlin'? I didn't mean to make you cry."

"I…Max. Our relationship is moving really fast. I mean…I—I'm worried that I'm feeling more than I should feel. I'm worried that I'm feeling more than is possible. But I'm sorry." Her breath caught. "My mom—even after my father's death—my mom and I, we were at odds for so many years. Because I was so resentful, so resentful of what the country had taken from me…they'd taken my dad, even before he was killed in action. And I was mad at my mom because my mom, she stood up for him. She stood up for him despite that he had put his country before us. She supported my father's decision; she supported the risk that he took. She took her loss of him with what I thought was too much acceptance. I didn't understand…until now."

Max pulled her head to his chest. His arms tightened around her.

"I didn't understand that she had loved him enough. Loved him for the man he was and the commitment he had made. That was the fabric of him. She had told me this oh so many times, in so many ways and I didn't understand." She looked up at him. "I do now. I hope that's not too much information."

A gentle smile curled at the corners of his lips.

"Kelsey, that's the most beautiful thing anyone has ever said to me. And I can understand how you felt. Thank you for telling me that. Thank you for feeling that. I'm experiencing an amazing feeling right now myself. Blessed beyond measure despite my circumstances with my military career and this knee. Holding you, it's more than I can believe. So no, you're not feeling things too quickly. I'm right there with you." He kissed her lips, then her temple and then her forehead and then he kissed her lips again.

He rested his cheek against her hair and just stood there. "Levi is taking me in the morning and if all goes well, I'll be out the following morning. So, I'll see you when I get out and, if all goes well, in two weeks I'll be up and starting to get to move around. I won't be a hundred percent but I'll be better than right now. I'll talk to you—"

"I can come to the surgery," she said, wanting to be there.

"No, it's okay. Levi will take me. I'm fine."

She felt disappointed that he didn't want her there, but she didn't push. "Okay then. I'll talk to you after surgery."

"I'll call you when I get home. Stay watchful and keep those doors locked. And if your ex-boss shows up, call 911 and they'll have someone here. Okay?"

"I'll be fine," she said.

"Call if you need them."

"Okay, I will."

"Go ahead and head inside and lock up. I'll wait until you're in."

It felt nice for him to be concerned but she didn't point out that she'd been taking care of herself for a very long time. Instead, she went inside and locked up and then waved from the window. Only then did he get in the truck and leave.

Kelsey prayed all would go well tomorrow. And as she got ready for bed, she still could not believe the emotions she was feeling.

She didn't hear from Max the next day. She went about her business and finally after lunch, she decided to call someone. Both Lana and Jessica were teaching school so she couldn't disturb them, so she called Shar.

"What's up, cowgirl? Thanks again for helping save the turtle the other day."

That made her smile. "I had a blast. Hey, um." She felt awkward asking. "I know Max had surgery this morning. Have you heard how he did?"

There was a pause. "So that's how it is," Shar said, a tease in her voice. "He did great. He's being released in the morning. The doctor said his knee was really destroyed and he had no idea how he'd managed the pain but he'll be better now. Crazy brother, keeping that from us that he was in such pain. Men! I tell you, sometimes you just want to pinch them. I told Gage he better not ever try to hide something like that from me or I'd cook his goose."

Kelsey laughed at that. Shar and Gage were really cute together. "I'm sure he couldn't and wouldn't want to hide something like that from you. Max is just really private."

"Yes, he is, but you obviously knew. That's a good sign. But don't feel bad that you haven't heard anything. Though he was awake and talking this afternoon, or so Levi told me, Max had told all of us that he didn't need a room full of family hovering at the hospital—it was just a knee. So we stayed away."

That made her feel a little better.

"So, you and Max. I like it."

"Oh, well, actually, we've just been talking."

"I was talking to a friend this morning who said she saw Max having dinner with someone night before last at the Paradise Grill. That wouldn't have been you, would it?"

"Yes. He wanted to have dinner before he went in for surgery."

"Like I said, I like it. My brother—he's very quiet, not one to talk about his private life much. You know, who he might be seeing or things like that. He stays holed up out there working on his place in between missions and sometimes the guys just have to go drag him out into the open. But that's Max. We were really startled when he agreed to do the Valentine auction and hopeful. Anyway, just warning you that he's not the easiest to get to know. He's all macho but a sweetheart. He doesn't want to bother anyone but he's dedicated beyond belief and well, he's a good guy. I'm really glad y'all are talking and I hope there's more to it than that."

Kelsey was smiling but didn't know what to say. "Thanks. Well, I'm glad he's doing good. I just want to make sure."

"He'll be home tomorrow. I'll update you if there's more."

"Thank you for the update. I need to get back to work now."

"Okay, me too. I'm glad you called. I'm sure you'll hear from him soon."

Kelsey was relieved as she ended the call and slipped her phone into her pocket. Shar had reiterated what she already knew: Max had walls and barriers built around him, even for his family. Probably stemming from the fact that on his missions, so much was kept secret and he couldn't tell anyone, share anything. It was worrisome. But that part of his life was over and now she hoped he could relax those walls. For a relationship to work, he would have to.

A truck drove into the drive and she could see the

family she was taking on a ride. She was thankful to be busy for the afternoon. She waved and headed toward them and placed thoughts of Max on the backburner…or at least she tried. She realized quickly that there was no putting Max in the background.

Thoughts of him followed her everywhere.

CHAPTER ELEVEN

Max was glad to be home.

"Okay, so you're good?" Levi asked after they got inside Max's house. "You're sure you don't need help?"

Max was on crutches. He looked over his shoulder at his brother. "I'm fine."

"You know, it's okay to ask for help."

"Sure, I know, but I'm fine. Thanks for taking me and getting me home. And for everything." He glanced over and saw food on the counter. And he knew his refrigerator would be full also. "I know that everyone is trying to take care of me but I'm okay. I can get around. I don't need to be coddled or…I just don't."

Levi smiled and shook his head. "Yes, sir." He looked understanding but skeptical. "Is there anything you want to tell me? Are you seeing someone?"

Max hopped around so he faced Levi. "Why do you ask?"

"Jessica called and told me that Shar had called her and told her that Kelsey had called, asking about you. She and your sisters are excited about the thought of the two of you maybe being an item."

He'd been feeling guilty for not calling Kelsey. Of course she would be worried. The fact that she'd called Shar to find out something showed him that she cared but he'd left her hanging. He was too used to keeping everything locked inside and to himself.

"Yeah, I took her out the night before surgery. Well, as good as I could take her out since I was in a fair amount of pain. But yeah, we're talking. She's really great." He said the last words thoughtfully.

His brother grinned. "I think that's good news. Your sisters are now really excited about this. So, you might be getting a little encouragement from their end. Just warning you."

Max did know his sisters. They had been getting into their brothers' business all their lives. Growing up with a bunch of romantic hearts had been something the guys had endured all their lives. Now he also had sisters-in-law to throw into the bundle.

"I think I need to call Kelsey. She's probably wondering why I haven't called."

"You should've called her yesterday. Not a good thing to leave her hanging like that. Shar felt bad for her, though she said Kelsey tried to act cool about the whole thing. There was a little bit of awkwardness at first. Jessica said Shar smoothed it over."

"Thanks for the heads-up. And thanks for having someone feed Charlotte—she appreciates it. I'll call if I need anything."

"Long as you call. That's all we ask."

After Levi left, Max eased down onto the couch and propped his leg up on the table beside the bottle of pain meds Levi had set within arm's reach. He still had a good bit in him from the hospital as he picked up his phone. He'd be taking it on a regular basis, supposedly. He hesitated before he dialed. He was used to taking care of himself, in the field and at home. He had to rely on himself. This letting people in was going to be something new.

He punched Kelsey's number. She deserved a call from him. "Hey, Kelsey," he said the minute she picked up. "It's me."

There was a long pause. "Hi. I guess you're home."

He heard the strain in her voice. *He'd messed up.* "Yeah, Levi just dropped me off. I'm on the couch now, still medicated with a few painkillers but I'm doing okay."

"I'm glad you're okay. I called Shar yesterday to make sure."

"Levi told me. Shar called Jessica and she said something to him. Now all my sisters—"

"I'm sorry if I inconvenienced you."

Her clipped words startled him.

He grimaced. "Kelsey, you didn't inconvenience me. I'm sorry. I should've called you. I should've told someone to give you an update. " *How did he go about this?* "Believe me, I feel bad. I'm wondering if you want to come out."

"I have a ride this afternoon."

His stomach tightened. Tension radiated between them, despite the painkillers in him. "Maybe this evening?"

Another long pause…then she sighed.

"Kelsey," he said, softly.

"I'll come out," she said at last. "If you're sure. But, Max, we'll need to talk."

Kelsey tried not to be mad. Told herself not to be. But she was.

She told herself that he'd just had surgery. That he was drugged and that he hadn't meant anything by not calling her. But there had been a hope inside her that maybe he would call at least later that evening after she'd called Shar. But he hadn't. And then this morning he hadn't called either. No, she'd had to wait until now. She glanced at her watch—two o'clock. He was home and he had finally decided to call her.

She knew they were just starting this relationship and maybe she shouldn't be upset but she was. She was opening her heart; she knew she was. There was no denying that her heart was going to be involved with Max Sinclair. And if he wasn't going to let her into his heart or his world in more ways than just telling her he was going to treat her like a lady, maybe they had two different ideas about what that was. If he cared about her, he would know that she needed to be included in things like this.

It was six thirty when she pulled into his drive. The gate was open. Well, at least she wasn't going to have to hop the fence and walk to his house. That was a good sign. But then again, it hadn't been him who'd left it open. No, she assumed it had been Levi. Max was going to have to start leaving his heart open, along with his gate.

She drove up to his house, angry and guilty for feeling angry. And mad and guilty for feeling mad. And upset and guilty for feeling upset. This was what it felt like to care for someone. She'd never felt this emotional rollercoaster. Oh, she'd had teenage angst growing up about boys she'd had crushes on. But this—this emotional connection with Max was all grown up emotions and something she was struggling with. There was a numbness inside her that had seeped into her with his silence and it was left over from what she felt after her dad died.

She had walls of her own.

And now she was about to let herself be vulnerable to hurt.

Her phone rang before she got out of the truck. She was in a hurry so she snatched it off the console and answered it on the second ring.

"Kelsey, I can't live without you."

Her mouth went dry at the sound of her ex-boss's voice. "Harrison, what are you doing?"

It was unimaginable that this man was acting like this. Yes, he had a control issue and had thought he could control her and manipulate her because she worked for him. But this was far over the top. "You tried to ruin me. I have no feelings for you. Leave me alone." She started to hang up.

"I want you, Kelsey. I love you," he said immediately. "I'm divorcing my wife—"

"Not for me," she snapped, completely sickened by the man. "I don't want anything to do with you. If you come near me again, this time I will press charges. Am I clear?"

She knew now that Max and Levi had been right. She shouldn't have let him off after attacking her in the grocery store parking lot. *What had she been thinking?* Clearly he had a problem and somehow she had become a fixation of his.

"I won't let someone else have you," he growled and then the line went dead.

Her pulse skittered…and her stomach soured with anger and bafflement rather than fear. If he thought he was going to push her around, he was mistaken. She got out of the truck and stalked to Max's door. Harrison was a control freak, obviously, but she had done nothing, absolutely nothing to warrant his odd behavior.

Trying to gather her wits, she took a deep breath and then tapped on Max's door.

"Come in."

She was happy to hear his voice and opened the door.

Max stood in the kitchen, leaning heavily on his crutches. His knee was in a brace and even from this distance, she saw strain in his face.

"Hey," he called, grinning at her as if he wasn't in pain.

She knew differently. She had been able to see past his façade almost from the beginning. "Max, you shouldn't be standing," she said instantly, forgetting everything but him in that moment.

"I'm fine. I'm warming up supper for us. My sisters and my mom delivered enough food to feed a small army."

She stalked across to the kitchen and stuffed her hands on her hips. "Max, you are the most stubborn man. I can fix my own food," she snapped. "You need to sit down. And when was the last time you took your pain meds?" She knew she sounded awful but she was done seeing him hurting. This was the last straw.

"I skipped it. I didn't want to be all medicated and

out of it when you got here."

"Max, you need it." She tried to keep her voice steady, to keep the emotions she was feeling for him inside. "Where is your pain medicine?"

"It's on the coffee table." He rested against the wall and leaned his head against it.

"Come on. Let's get you back to the couch." She placed an arm around his waist and he looked down at her.

"You're angry at me."

"More frustrated than anything," she said, sternly. "After the other night, you should have call—"

He stopped her words with a kiss; his arm slid around her waist and pulled her close while his mouth moved over hers.

She stiffened, tried to resist the emotions melting her knees and her resolve, and then she was kissing him back. Losing herself in the wonder and joy of his touch.

"I'm sorry," he muttered against her lips at last before he pulled away to look at her. "I should have let you in. I told you I was going to. I told you I was going to treat you right and I didn't. It's not a good way to start our relationship."

Her heart had been hurting with his lack of including her, of not letting her past his barriers but now, she felt as if they'd made a step forward. "This…what is happening between us…has to be a partnership. I've given it a lot of thought and you…you spent most of your life having to keep your life to yourself. You haven't had anyone other than your team members to talk to. But now it's a new time…and for a relationship to work, we'll need to be a team. You and me."

"I like that."

"You have to let me in. And I get that we just started this. But if you can't let me in now, I'm afraid you might not let me later. And Max, I have my own baggage, my own insecurities and barriers to overcome and I can't risk my heart with so little. No matter how much I care for you."

"I understand. I agree." He kissed her again.

He agreed.

His hand cupped her face gently. One of the

crutches fell to the ground, making a horrible crashing sound, and they both jumped. "Sorry about that. That's enough to wake us both up."

She chuckled. "Or give us a heart attack," she said. "I care about you, Max."

"And I care about you. I'm falling in love with you, Kelsey."

She closed her eyes. His words sunk into the dark space inside her heart. A space that had been dark and lonely for so long. She opened her eyes. "That's how I feel. I'm falling for you, too, Max." She'd already fallen.

"Then are you going to give us a chance? It looks like I have a few things to learn. But I want to. You're worth it, Kelsey. Can we start from here?"

She knew there was no way she was going to say anything but yes. At least he knew how she felt. "Yes. Now you have to sit down. I'm going to give you a pain pill and you're not going to feel any pain for a while." She picked up his crutch and helped him over to the couch.

Then she picked up his medication and read the

instructions, shook out one pill and handed it to him along with the glass of water from the table. "Take this."

He did exactly as she asked. "It looks like you're learning," she said as he swallowed the pill.

"Yes, ma'am. I'm going to try."

She laughed and it felt so wonderful. "All right. I'm going to go finish what you were fixing in there while you relax."

"Yes, nurse."

By the time she had the casserole heated up, he was sleeping. She sank down into the chair and watched him sleep. All the tension that had been in his expression was relaxed. Her heart swelled with fullness and…love.

CHAPTER TWELVE

The sun coming up through his window woke Max. He was still on the couch, with a blanket over him. On the table next to him was a tray with some of the blueberry muffins—his favorite—that his mother had brought over before he'd come home from the hospital. There was a container of them on the kitchen counter. Kelsey had also poured some orange juice in a glass and a cup of coffee in an insulated cup. And there was a note, neatly folded beside the plate.

I hope you slept well. You woke once and took another round of medicine. I left at seven to get ready for work. Call if you need anything. There's more coffee brewing in the coffee maker. Kelsey

He fingered the note and wished he'd wakened thirty minutes earlier. He didn't remembered passing out on Kelsey or waking up to take more medicine. His stomach rumbled, reminding him that he hadn't even made it through dinner. She'd had to eat by herself and then what—sit in the chair and watch him snore? He rubbed his neck. "What a great night Kelsey must have had," he grumbled.

He was so ready to be done with this knee. Frustration had him sitting up. He picked up his crutches and ignored the throb in his knee as he maneuvered up to a standing position. He balanced there on the crutches and then reached down and picked up the coffee. She'd taken the time to fix this and he needed something to take the fuzz out of his brain. He took a long swallow of the still hot coffee and then another. Finally he set it back down and headed to the shower, only to remember he couldn't yet get his leg wet. He turned the shower on and balancing, he stuck his head in. He needed clarity. He wouldn't be taking any more pain medicine.

An hour later, when the medicine was completely gone and the pain that radiated from his knee told him he was back to being fully in control of all his senses, Max headed out to the truck. It was time to see Kelsey again.

Kelsey was brushing down Rip, one of the big bay geldings, when she heard the crunch of boots. She was tired, after sitting up in a chair most of the night. She hadn't wanted to leave Max. She'd sat there and watched over him while she watched old movies on the television. It had felt good looking out for him. But it was Saturday and she'd had to come back to the stables and get ready for her morning class of kids. She was expecting to see one of them, maybe Kevin, when she looked up but it was the last person she'd expected to see…

"Max." She gasped and dropped the brush and stood up. "What are you doing?"

He smiled, the dimple showing immediately. "I

came to tell you how much I enjoyed you coming over last night."

She knew she should be mad at him for disobeying the doctor's orders again but her heart was dipping with the disbelief and the joy that he'd wanted to come see her so badly. Still, concern for him beat out everything. "Max, you shouldn't have. You need to be at home. This can't be good for your knee. And what about the painkillers? Are you drivin—"

"I haven't taken any since you gave it to me this morning. I have a high pain tolerance but I'm told when I go for therapy that I'll have to have it. Jake is taking me for that at nine and I wanted to talk to you before that because who knows—I might be sleeping again—which I hate."

She knew he did; she could feel his frustrations. Max was an active guy who'd been sidelined by this injury. She moved to him and cupped his cheek. "You're going to be over all this in a few weeks and back up to speed."

He wrapped an arm around her waist and pulled her close. "I didn't think you were ever going to come out of that stall. I'm going to work those therapists out. I'm getting this knee well as fast as possible. Cam and Lana will be getting married in May and I'm needing a date and a dance partner—but not just anyone. I want it to be you." He hitched a brow.

"That sounds like a great idea. I'd love that."

The sound of a vehicle driving into the yard had his arm tightening around her. "Then it's a date." He kissed her gently. "Then I'm a happy man. I'll head back home and wait for Jake. This waiting around for people is driving me crazy."

"Patience is obviously not your strong point."

"No. It's not. I'll call you." He kissed her quickly as the sound of kids and the slamming of car doors could be heard. "Sounds like we've got company."

"Jessica is bringing Kevin and his friends to ride."

"Oh, sounds fun. He's a cute kid."

"Yes, he is."

She pulled out of his arms and let him get situated with the crutches and start moving. She could see it hurt him but the man was amazing where pain tolerance was concerned.

Kevin rounded the corner with his buddies and skidded to a halt. "Max, cool. You've got crutches."

She bit back a grin. *Leave it to kids to think crutches were cool.*

"Hey, buddy. I do have them. Give me a few weeks and you can have these if you want them."

Kevin looked at the other guys and beamed. "Awesome. You guys can use them too."

Jessica approached them and shook her head. "You've made his day. Of course, I'm not sure what Mr. Short Stuff thinks he's going to do with your tall crutches."

"I'm sure he'll figure something out. I'll just be glad to be rid of them."

"I'll like them," Kevin said. "I might need them when I grow up."

"This is true," Max agreed. "All I can say is they're yours when the doc says I can toss them to the curb, so get ready." He turned to Kelsey. "I need to go. Jake will not be happy if he gets to my house and can't find me."

"Levi isn't going to believe it when I tell him you

are already up and about. Are you supposed to be driving?"

His lip lifted into a lopsided grin. "I had something important to take care of. I'll call you, Kelsey."

"Please be careful."

"Sure thing."

"See you later, fellas," he called to the kids. They all waved and yelled bye to him as he headed to his truck.

She felt her phone vibrate in her pocket and pulled it out to glance at the screen. *Harrison.* She ignored the call. She'd thought about telling Max about his call last night but it hadn't been the place and then Max had fallen asleep. She'd tell him later but for now she would ignore him. With any luck, he'd get the message and leave her alone.

She told the boys to get their horses, which she had tied in their stalls.

Jessica looked at her with smiling eyes. "So, he came to see you? How interesting."

"Is Levi as stubborn as his brother?"

"Oh, I think so. I have a feeling he wouldn't be a very good patient if he was in a situation like Max. But you just sidestepped my observation. He looked really happy and any pain looked insignificant in the face of the way he looked at you."

Kelsey took a deep breath. "Oh Jess, I think he and I just moved into some serious relationship waters."

"I think that's wonderful. I know Levi was really happy at the thought of you two being an item."

That made her happy, knowing everyone was so thrilled about her and Max.

But the best part was that she was happy about it. And still couldn't quite believe it.

Max lived through physical therapy over the next week. He decided that Phyllis, his therapist, was actually a Marine sergeant in disguise. She was one tough cookie and planned to help him recover as much stability in his knee as possible. Kelsey came in the evenings and she helped him to have patience with his recovery. If it hadn't been for her, he would not have stayed put. But spending time with her just relaxing was the best possible thing to help keep him from overdoing.

On the fourth night, he knew he never wanted his life to be without her. He was pretty sure Charlotte felt the same way. His pig loved Kelsey and knew the sound of her truck. He understood how she felt. If he could run to her, he would.

One thing he knew above all else was he was not ever going to let her down. And he planned to do his best to win her love for the rest of his life.

CHAPTER THIRTEEN

The next three weeks passed in a blur. Max was involved in therapy and he went every day that he was supposed to and did his own workouts to improve. He called Kelsey and came to see her almost every day. For Kelsey, it was a time of happiness and some disbelief at wondering how she could be so lucky to have found Max. He was everything she could hope for and though she could tell he still had moments when he regretted not being able to go back to his missions, right now his sole focus was on getting better as fast as he could.

She hadn't heard from Harrison again and was glad she hadn't ever found the right time to mention it to Max. With his injury, she hadn't wanted to worry him.

Tonight, as she was headed out to his place, she was excited. He'd said he had a surprise and she was curious. Excited and so ready to spend time with him, she drove along the winding road toward his place. It was dark as she neared his drive. The truck that was behind her got right on her bumper, its bright lights blinding in the rearview. She turned onto the road, quicker than she should, and fishtailed as her tires hit the gravel. "Goodness, fella," she muttered as she slammed on her brakes.

The truck slowed and then gassed it before it disappeared down the road. Her heart thundered as she drove through the open gate and headed down the lane to Max's house.

He stood outside the bungalow, wearing shorts and the knee brace. He had been able to get rid of the crutches and was moving around so much better. Everyone in the family now knew they were a steady couple and they were all supportive, although Max remained private and preferred their spending time alone. But she was fine with that because she enjoyed their time alone. She pushed the thoughts of the truck out of her mind—looking at Max was enough to wipe out the thought of over-aggressive drivers.

Charlotte trotted to her, grunting and wiggling all over. Bending down, she rubbed the large pig's ears and grinned at Max. "This little pig has had a bath…how did you get that accomplished?"

He chuckled. "Charlotte is like a dog who loves a shower. All I have to do is turn it on and open the door, and she's in there. I dried her off so she would be nice and clean when you got here."

"Well, you are looking mighty nice," she said to the pig. "And so are you. You look like you're doing a lot better."

"I am." He leaned against the wall and crossed his arms. "It won't be long and I'm tossing this brace."

"Sounding pretty cocky there." She rose and moved toward him. He opened his arms and she stepped into his hug. She looked forward to this all day. And knew she would never, ever get tired of feeling his arms around her.

"I've missed you," he said. "And you smell good—washed that horse right off yourself?"

She laughed. "Yes, I did. As always."

"I like you any way you are but I have to admit soft floral is better than horse. Come on, let's get in the ATV. I've got something to show you."

"My surprise?"

"Yes." He took her hand and led her to the ATV. There was no doubt that he was moving better. "Stay here, Charlotte," he told the pig and immediately she moved to sit on the doorstep to wait.

He drove up the rutted path toward the house. He pulled to a stop. "Stay put," he said, his grin sending a shiver of happiness through her. "Wait for me."

Moving slower than she knew he wanted to, he came around to her and took her hand. She had a feeling that when Max's brace came off, the man would be a mass of energy.

The warmth of his touch sent tingles of awareness pulsing over her and anticipation to what he had waiting for inside his house.

When they walked inside, there was a table set for two. Candles flickered softly and romantic music played. She gasped. "Oh Max, this is so romantic." And it was. Through the window, the soft moonlit water was visibleadding to the beautiful setting.

"I wanted this to be special." He looked into her eyes.

Her heart fluttered. She had never had anyone do a romantic dinner for her. "This is lovely and unexpected." Her heart clutched in her chest with love for this guy.

She couldn't help it. She knew that he was the man for her.

There were no obstacles between them. He led her over to the table and took her into his arms. And then he lowered his head and kissed her with a deep tenderness that caused her world to spin and color to blossom through her.

At last he said, "I haven't worked on the house since the last time you came here. So there still a ton of stuff that has to be done. I have blueprints, but the plans can be altered. In my own life, I've learned that sometimes what we want can change. I've learned to adapt and move forward. And I've learned that the new future can be a blessing. You helped me see that. You were here for me when I was at my worst, Kelsey. I don't think anybody knows how hard this injury and the loss of my buddies has been on me. But you knew. You sensed it and you saw it. And even though you had been through so much, with losing your dad and the thought of me being in the military was hard on you, you were still there for me. And I'll never forget that."

He paused and kissed her hand. "I love you, Kelsey. I have been falling for you from the first day I saw you in the stables there at Cam's place."

Kelsey's knees had gone weak.

"When I saw you at the engagement party and I asked the guys who you were, Cam told me you were his manager. I couldn't help myself. I had to come out there to meet you. But I never dreamed that I was meeting the one. I just knew that something about you—your energy, your smile...something compelled me to come out there that next day and meet you. It was a shock how strong the pull of you was to me. I never dreamed that you were the one. I didn't know—I just knew that I had to be near you and every day since you have captivated me."

Kelsey felt tears prick at the corners of her eyes. *He loved her.* And he had told her so. She'd had to fight every instinct that told her to leave him, to walk away from everything he was and represented. But she had been unable to do that. Unable to listen to the warnings. Her heart seemed to have known before anything else that this was a man she could not walk away from.

"I love you too, Max. It's been almost the same journey for me. I've learned that sometimes you can love so much that you are able to go against what your logic is telling you and you are able to embrace, or tolerate, something that you didn't think you could because the other person is so dedicated to it. And that is part of that person you love. I'm pretty sure that's how my mom felt about my dad, and I could not understand that until you."

He was quiet for a moment and she could tell he was thinking. "I loved it," he said after a moment. "And I served proudly and with all my heart for this country. But, Kelsey, now it's a new chapter in my life. And I want you in it."

Kelsey gasped when he pulled a chair out and sank down into it. Still holding her hand, he looked up at her.

"I can't get on my knee. Not yet, anyway." He grinned sheepishly. "But I can't wait any longer. I can't wait another three or four weeks before that's possible. I want to ask you now if you'll marry me. Will you, Kelsey Malone, be my wife?"

She couldn't breathe. Her heart shot into the stratosphere as her heart thundered and her knees melted to mush. "Yes," she croaked through tears. "I want that so much. You have worked so hard to open up and I want to share my life with you."

His eyes looked bright as he stood. "You have just made my life beautiful. I am honored." He wrapped her in his arms and kissed her deeply, passionately, and she could feel the love in his kiss. She felt the promise of tomorrow and every day after that in his kiss.

Finally smiling, he pulled away and reached down to lift a napkin from the table to reveal a small jeweler's box beneath it. He picked it up and then lifted the lid. "If you don't like this, there's plenty more where it came from. We'll go and pick out whatever you want."

She stared at the beautiful, exquisite diamond ring glittering in the candlelight. The beautiful princess cut diamond was set in platinum and surrounded by a circle of diamonds.

"I wanted the ring of diamonds around the solitaire to symbolize that my love for you is never ending and that it will always encircle you. From this day forward, you are the center of my life and my love will always encircle you and cherish you."

She was crying now. "It's perfect. I adore it. I adore you." And then she threw herself into his arms and kissed him.

Suddenly, an awful noise ripped through the evening air. Kelsey jumped. The sound hadn't been far from the house.

"Was that Charlotte?"

Max had already turned in the direction of the front of the house. He was on full alert. "It was Charlotte. Someone is here."

"But she sounded like she was in pain."

He nodded and his expression had hardened. Max had gone from lover to warrior in an instant. Moving as fast as he could, he moved to the window. She started to follow him but he held up his hand.

"She's not making any more noise," Kelsey gasped.

"Kelsey, blow those candles out."

She didn't hesitate as she spun back to the table and blew the flickering candles out. Darkness instantly surrounded them. He took her hand in the darkness. "This way."

He led her toward the kitchen area, where there were walls, and he pushed her gently into the alcove where the refrigerator would go. "Stay there, in the back," he whispered. "I need to know where you are. Something doesn't feel right."

"But I don't understand."

She heard a crunch of gravel. He heard it too. "Stay put."

And then he was gone. Her heart pounded. Her eyes had adjusted to the darkness and she was making out forms of studs and unfinished wall frames. Unable to stop herself, she moved to the edge of the opening and peeked around the corner, searching for Max. She saw a dark shadow of someone move into the house. *Who?*

Her stomach felt sick with fear. *What had happened to Charlotte? What was going on?*

Where was Max? Suddenly, a spotlight of light shot through the darkness and illuminated…her ex-boss. She gasped…and then she saw the gun.

Her gaze swept from him to where the spotlight was. It was propped on a workbench but Max wasn't there. Harrison glanced too; he only saw the light and then he focused back on her.

"Move out here, Kelsey. I came for you. I can't take it. I need you. I can't let you go."

She had known Harrison was obsessive. Had seen his tendency to go to extremes to always get what he wanted but she'd never dreamed he would take that obsession and apply it to her. *Where was Max?* Fear for him shrouded her. She stepped out into the open.

"Harrison, you need to put that gun away."

He waved it. "I'll hang onto it, if it's all the same to you. Come here and your boyfriend might not get hurt."

"Stay right where you are," Max demanded. "You are not getting your hands on her. Kelsey, call Levi. Dial 911, now."

Her phone was in her pocket, thank goodness. Her hands shook as she pulled it out and managed to punch the numbers with trembling fingers. The dispatcher answered as Harrison managed to connect a fist to Max's jaw. Max got a hit in and then in a split second, he flipped Harrison over. The gun skidded across the floor. Max yanked Harrison's hands up into his shoulder blades.

She immediately moved toward the gun just as Harrison kicked Max in his bad knee. Max grunted and lost hold of Harrison's wrist; in the next minute, Harrison was on top of Max. She had the gun.

"Stop," she yelled just as an awful sound erupted and Charlotte blasted into the house. Blood dripped down the poor pig's head. She was a rotund flash as she let out a war cry and charged Harrison, slamming into him with all her considerable weight. Immediately Harrison was on the ground, his head slamming against the cement. He went limp as the pig sat on his chest and glared down at him.

Max rolled away and struggled to stand. She hurried to help him and he pulled her to his side. Both of them kept their eyes on Harrison, who remained still. Charlotte continued to sit solidly on top of his back, staring at them as if to say she had it under control.

"Are you okay?" he asked.

"I'm fine. Terrified. Are you okay? How is your knee?"

"I'll live. But it didn't help me in that fight."

She hugged him, so relieved he was okay. "I was so worried. He's crazy!"

"He's got problems but he's about to have time to work through them because this time charges are being filed."

She agreed. "I'll press them this time."

"Good for you. But I'm pressing them too. He came in here to harm you and that is never happening again." He pulled her close and kissed her forehead. Sirens could be heard in the distance.

"Charlotte, you're doing a great job, sweetie pie."

The pig grunted and then, as if to say she could do better, Charlotte stretched out on top of Harrison's chest and let out a long, loud grunt before laying her snout against his cheek.

"This isn't exactly the romantic evening that I had envisioned," Max said.

She cupped his cheek with her palm and smiled. "But we're both safe. And nothing that has happened has changed the fact that I'm going to be your wife."

He kissed her. "And that means I'm still the happiest and luckiest man alive."

Excerpt from

WITH THIS WISH

Windswept Bay, Book Nine

CHAPTER ONE

The wind blew hot and humid across Trent Sinclair as he rode his Harley along the curving shoreline road of Windswept Bay. He had been rebuilding this vintage Knucklehead Harley for two years and now it purred like a big kitten. Knowing he'd rebuilt it with his own hands was a rewarding feeling. It gave him a sense of accomplishment.

It had also kept him busy in the evenings.

Kept his mind busy and he needed that after he'd

been released from the military and special ops. He hadn't managed well when he first came home almost three years ago and finding the bike several months after arriving had been a lifeline that he'd needed. He hadn't wanted to hang out, or go out at all. Other than seeing his family—his brothers and sisters—most of the time after he finished work, he'd just wanted time alone. But he'd found too much time spent with nothing but the sound of crickets, frogs, and even the sound of the small waterfall not too far away through the trees didn't work well for him... It enabled too much time for memories, regrets, and stagnation.

He'd realized he needed something to help him mark time and working on the Harley had been exactly the right project. But now it was finished. And time had moved on, life had moved on... But was he ready?

Had his heart healed enough? Did he want to reach for more?

There was no hurry. Now, he'd take pleasure in this—riding, feeling the life that vibrated in the air as he rode the Harley. For now, that was what he'd focus on. That and taking one step at a time toward moving forward at last.

He studied the surf as he followed the curve of the road and thought how lucky he was to live in such a beautiful spot. He turned onto the secluded road that led up the hillside and away from the blue waters of the bay. He enjoyed the seclusion of his tree-surrounded home away from the surf, contrary to what most people wanted out of a home near the beach. As he wound up the hill and rounded the last curve to his driveway, he had to yank the bike hard to the left to miss the baby-blue travel trailer blocking the road.

The bike skidded and he managed to miss a tree as he careened through the ditch, caught air and skidded to a halt in his driveway. He cut the ignition and dropped the kickstand to the Knucklehead.

Who... What?

The questions blasted through him as he glared toward the faded Chevy attached to the small egg-shaped travel trailer that blocked his drive and the road. Anger flashed through him as he scanned the area, no one was there.

"Are you all right?"

He yanked his head around and saw a blonde standing halfway between him and the house, a look of shock on her tanned face. What little he could see of her face for the mass of hair.

"What are you thinking?" he demanded as he hauled off the bike and strode toward her. "You trying to get someone killed with that rig of yours?"

"No. I thought it was off the road enough. I have my flashers on."

"Nope, no flashers and not off the road enough."

She pushed curls from her face with one hand and left her hand on her forehead, as if to hold the mass back. Her brow wrinkled above her dark shades. "Well, I'll move it. I was under the impression there was little traffic from here on up the hillside."

"True enough, but still not a good thing. You should have moved it at least out of the way of the curve and my driveway."

"Fine. I'll move it and be right back." She jogged past him in an easy stride.

He set his hands on his hips and watched as she yanked open the passenger door, slid inside, and then yanked it closed. She scooted to the driver's seat and gunned the engine. A loud backfire boomed from the old truck before it lunged forward and towed the blue egg across his driveway and up the road ten feet past the entrance of his home. That was one ugly little trailer.

But one really cute owner, he noticed as within moments, she was jogging back his way. Her hair seemed alive as she loped up his asphalt and stopped in front of him. She pulled her shades off, exposing her pretty, makeup-less skin and sparkling eyes the color of periwinkles that grew in his mother's window boxes. She let her hand holding the shades drop to her thigh and his gaze followed the movement, past her T-shirt with Yosemite National Park scrawled across her small breasts, to a pair of cutoff jeans that hit just above mid-thigh on her tanned, well-toned legs. His gaze snagged on the shades as she tapped them on the side of her thigh near the long, jagged scar that ran down the side of her left leg. The scar had been hidden from his view as she'd jogged past on her way to the truck but now, though faded, it was an obvious leftover from what he envisioned as a painful accident or surgery.

"So, now that I have that out of the way, we can talk."

Her happy voice had him yanking his gaze off her legs back to meet her clear gaze. She smiled and instantly went from pretty to knockout in one swift kick in the gut.

"Talk?" he muttered, struggling to pull his attention from the pain of her injury to the happy lilt of her tone and those eyes. *That smile. It was completely disconcerting.*

"Yes, first, I love your ride. A real beauty." She turned to look at the Knucklehead and his gaze snagged again on the vicious scar. It was faded but from this angle clearly had once, years ago, been terrible.

Trent's thoughts went back momentarily to a time he tried hard not to remember. He shook his head and forced his attention to his Harley. "Thanks. I like it."

She turned back, her smile wide. "I hope you'll give me a ride at some point. I can only imagine the freedom of it. And I'm sure it purrs smooth as butter as you ride."

His concentration faltered at her words. "You know vintage bikes?" As startling as every second since he'd come up on her was the instant attraction that shot through him. His mind faltered because it had been awhile since he'd been instantly attracted to someone…not since Erica. Thinking of Erica, he forced himself to focus on the intriguing woman. On finding out who she was and why she was here.

"I don't really know them. I've just been around a lot of motorcycles and a vintage bike stands out." Lilly McCall took in the gorgeous guy in front of her. He stood out, too, more than his motorcycle. He was tall, lean and hard muscle and though she'd done her research on him before, she hadn't been prepared for the unexpected attraction buzzing through her. That could be a problem. "I'm Lilly McCall," she said, realizing she'd never introduced herself.

"I'm Trent Sinclair, but I have a feeling you

already know that." His head cocked. "McCall. Wait, are you my brother-in-law BJ's sister?"

She nodded. "I am. But he has no idea I'm here yet." She extended her hand and she saw her reflection in his aviators and could see her crazy hair was pretty wild from the salt air and the fact that she'd been riding with the windows open for the last four hours. She was a bit of a mess with it having expanded to twice its normal size. *Oh well, it was what it was.*

He took her hand and shook in a firm, professional manner. She liked the feel of his callused palm though it was a very brief handshake. "Are you lost?"

She smiled. "No, I know exactly where I'm at."

He removed his aviators and her heart skipped a beat as striking blue eyes the color of the teal-toned water of the coast met hers.

"So, you came to see me?" His gaze locked onto hers, probing.

Awareness churned in her chest and she fought it off like a woman fighting off bees. The man was as sexy as the heroes of the books she wrote and she couldn't have written a heroine's reaction any better than her reaction to him.

"Well, in part but I'm also on my way to my place."

He crossed his arms—his distractingly muscled arms—and his brows dipped. "Your place?"

She was confusing him. She did tend to do that. *Focus, Lilly.* "I'm here about a treehouse. I want you to build me one."

He hitched an eyebrow. "You know about my treehouses?"

"I do. I was talking to BJ a month ago and he was telling me what each of his new brothers-in-law do. And he mentioned that you'd been building treehouses. And, well, I started thinking about it and couldn't let the idea go. So, here I am and I'd like you to build me one. If you have time. And I'm really hoping you do." She really did. She was set on it, actually. This move she was making was huge for her. Deciding to take hold of her life and set down roots. It was big. It was hard and the whimsical idea of living in a treehouse had taken hold of her like a vise and wouldn't let go. She wanted this treehouse. *Truly wanted to plant roots and stay…*

"Where? Don't you travel around a lot? Like from one national park to the other or something like that?"

Her heart tugged. "I do. I mean, I did. I'm starting a new chapter in my life, though. I'm…" She moistened her lips and the soles of her feet suddenly itched. "I'm settling down. Here on Windswept Bay. BJ is here."

"Well, I think that's great. He didn't mention you were coming last time I talked to him."

"He doesn't know."

Trent looked shocked now. "Really, you're surprising him?"

"Yes, I am." She hadn't wanted anyone to know her plan. She'd made it, was used to making decisions on her own and flying by the seat of her pants. "I'm going to see him but I wanted to settle in first and get things with the treehouse rolling."

"Rolling?"

"Yes. Can you fit a treehouse into your schedule over the next few months?"

He placed his hands on his jean-clad hips and

studied her with real consternation now. "Well, I am finishing up a remodel in a couple of days but I have another job scheduled in two months."

"Great. That's plenty of time, isn't it?"

He laughed. "Maybe. Depends on how extravagant you want it."

"Nice, but not extravagant. I'm not an extravagant kind of person."

"Okay, so where is the spot? I'll need to look at it."

"Fantastic. It's just around the corner, up the hill."

He blinked. "This hill?"

She nodded as if she hadn't said anything startling, but she had. "Yes, up the road."

"*You* bought the property at the top of this hill?"

Lilly shouldn't have been surprised by his reaction. Of course he would know what the property at the top of this hill would cost. He lived right here mid-way up the road to it.

"I did." And his reaction was right, the property

hadn't come cheap. She wondered what was going through his mind. Probably thought she had a loan from BJ. The truth was far from that. "Look, I'll pay whatever you want, if that's what's worrying you. But I do have a deadline. I need it within the next two months."

"Okay, but you're sure you want a treehouse up *there*? This is the Florida coast and we do have hurricanes from time to time."

"I'm sure. I'll deal with the hurricanes when they come. But I know what I want. Can you do it? I've checked out your work and love it." She placed her hands on her hips and prepared herself to convince him to do this, no matter what it took. "I know what I want and you can give that to me."

His brow rose and the suggestive connotation of her words slammed into her. Being a twenty-six-year-old phenomenon who hid inside her volunteer work inside the national park service slightly hindered her love life. And there was the fact that a knot lived inside her that couldn't—wouldn't—loosen its hold on her heart. She could write her quirky, sweet romances but to actually open up to them herself was something she didn't think she would ever be able to do.

So she just wrote love stories…there was no threat of pain if she let that be enough. Truth was, there had never been any attraction toward someone who challenged her heart.

He was staring at her and she realized he'd never answered. "Look, are you the man for the job?"

His lips twitched and his eyes crinkled at the edges. "I might be. I'll have to take a look at the property first. Maybe we should drive up there and take a look at what exactly you want in this slightly restrictive scenario you've just described."

She laughed with relief. She had him and she knew it. "Great! Let's go. Your ride or mine?"

More Books by Debra Clopton

Star Gazer Inn of Corpus Christi Bay
What New Beginnings are Made of (Book 1)
What Dreams are Made of (Book 2)
What Hopes are Made of (Book 3)
What a Heart's Desire is Made of (Book 4)
What True Love is Made of (Book 5)

Sunset Bay Romance
Longing for Forever (Book 1)
Longing for a Hero (Book 2)
Longing for Love (Book 3)
Longing for Ever After (Book 4)
Longing for You (Book 5)
Longing for Us (Book 6)

Texas Brides & Bachelors
Heart of a Cowboy (Book 1)
Trust of a Cowboy (Book 2)
True Love of a Cowboy (Book 3)

New Horizon Ranch Series
Her Texas Cowboy: Cliff (Book 1)
Rescued by Her Cowboy: Rafe (Book 2)
Protected by Her Cowboy: Chase (Book 3)
Loving Her Best Friend Cowboy: Ty (Book 4)
Family for a Cowboy: Dalton (Book 5)
The Mission of Her Cowboy: Treb (Book 6)
Maddie's Secret Baby (Book 7)
This Cowgirl Loves This Cowboy: Austin (Book 8)

Turner Creek Ranch Series
Treasure Me, Cowboy (Book 1)
Rescue Me, Cowboy (Book 2)
Complete Me, Cowboy (Book 3)
Sweet Talk Me, Cowboy (Book 4)

Cowboys of Ransom Creek
Her Cowboy Hero (Book 1)
The Cowboy's Bride for Hire (Book 2)
Cooper: Charmed by the Cowboy (Book 3)
Shane: The Cowboy's Junk-Store Princess (Book 4)
Vance: Her Second-Chance Cowboy (Book 5)
Drake: The Cowboy and Maisy Love (Book 6)
Brice: Not Quite Looking for a Family (Book 7)

Texas Matchmaker Series
Dream With Me, Cowboy (Book 1)
Be My Love, Cowboy (Book 2)
This Heart's Yours, Cowboy (Book 3)
Hold Me, Cowboy (Book 4)
Be Mine, Cowboy (Book 5)
Operation: Married by Christmas (Book 6)
Cherish Me, Cowboy (Book 7)
Surprise Me, Cowboy (Book 8)
Serenade Me, Cowboy (Book 9)
Return To Me, Cowboy (Book 10)
Love Me, Cowboy (Book 11)
Ride With Me, Cowboy (Book 12)
Dance With Me, Cowboy (Book 13)

Windswept Bay Series
From This Moment On (Book 1)
Somewhere With You (Book 2)
With This Kiss (Book 3)
Forever and For Always (Book 4)
Holding Out For Love (Book 5)
With This Ring (Book 6)
With This Promise (Book 7)
With This Pledge (Book 8)
With This Wish (Book 9)
With This Forever (Book 10)
With This Vow (Book 11)

About the Author

Bestselling author Debra Clopton has sold over 2.5 million books. Her book OPERATION: MARRIED BY CHRISTMAS has been optioned for an ABC Family Movie. Debra is known for her contemporary, western romances, Texas cowboys and feisty heroines. Sweet romance and humor are always intertwined to make readers smile. A sixth generation Texan she lives with her husband on a ranch deep in the heart of Texas. She loves being contacted by readers.

Visit Debra's website at www.debraclopton.com

Sign up for Debra's newsletter at www.debraclopton.com/contest/

Check out her Facebook at www.facebook.com/debra.clopton.5

Follow her on Twitter at @debraclopton

Contact her at debraclopton@ymail.com

If you enjoyed reading *With This Pledge* I would appreciate it if you would help others enjoy this book, too.

Recommend it. Please help other readers find this book by recommending it to friends, reader's groups and discussion boards.

Review it. Please tell other readers why you liked this book by reviewing it on the retail site you purchased it from or Goodreads. If you do write a review, please send an email to debraclopton@ymail.com so I can thank you with a personal email. Or visit me at: www.debraclopton.com.